I0671476

Serpents in the Temple

The Revered Mother Of Prymiah, Volume 2

Addison Foxx

Published by Strange Planet Publications, 2022.

SERPENTS IN THE TEMPLE

First edition. February 15, 2022.

Copyright © 2022 Addison Foxx.

ISBN: 978-1737783848

Written by Addison Foxx.

"The enemy's assumption of your weakness is your greatest weapon. The proof of their error is in their defeat."

-Shaed Elrek, Vok-tor Master, and Temple Warrior

This volume is dedicated with love, to HDM.

It is as it shoud be.

A.

CHAPTER ONE

ALEX COULDN'T BELIEVE he found himself in this position again. Right where he didn't want to be. Oh he was at home all right. And sitting right in front of him was that old tomcat Jyn-Shaed. And to add insult to injury, there was his mother, as beautiful as ever, sitting right next to her rapist.

Morgan could see the look on her son's face, and so could Lindsey.

'Mom, could you help me in the kitchen? Everyone must be hungry.'

'Sure, Lindsey, be glad to. I need to check the bird. The Prymiahns don't eat much meat, but Alex likes meat, and he likes it tender, so I'm cooking for him especially.'

Morgan knew what was coming, and she didn't want to see it. Alex had gotten better with his anger, but not by much. This was going to be Alex's last day on Earth for a while, and he wasn't taking it well. Jyn said:

'Alex, can't we just get along for you mother's sake?'

'It's not that, you old tomcat. I know my mother. And I know what she's capable of enduring to save her family.'

'Then what is it, Alex?'

'I don't want to leave my home. This is all I've ever known. I don't know what's waiting for me out there. You people have taken everything from us.'

'You'll have a new home, Alex. But you aren't leaving Earth forever. And not only that, but your whole family is also going with you. I don't expect you to like it. And it will be strange for you. Our planet will seduce you. It hoards its own people and when newcomers arrive, it hoards them too. It's hard to describe. You will leave it soon enough so you can continue your rebellion. But you'll ache for it, just like you now ache for Earth before you've even left.'

'I hate you.'

'I know.'

MORGAN AND LINDSEY began putting food on the table, and Mandy had gotten up from her nap. She looked curiously at Jyn, who was dressed more like a Terran today, but chose to wear his long hair in his Warrior's ponytail. Mandy, who was even more curious than her grandmother, immediately climbed up on Jyn's lap and began pulling his ponytail, much to his delight. Alex cringed at this, but Lindsey and Morgan loved seeing it because they knew that Mandy was comfortable with her alien grandfather, and he looked comfortable with her.

'Reminds me of my girls at that age. Always pulling at my hair.'

At that moment, Mandy stood up on Jyn's lap and pulled at his mouth, revealing his sharp canines. 'Mommy, Poppow got kitty teeth! Myoww, myoww!'

Morgan and Lindsey got a great laugh at this, but Alex stopped eating and was trying too hard not to chuckle at his little girl. But he had always delighted in her. She reminded him of his mom and now she was all over Jyn's mouth looking at all his teeth. After she was satisfied, she jumped down, running all over the house shouting '*Myoww, myoww*!' everywhere she went.

After everyone had finished eating, it became very quiet. Mandy had crawled up on Jyn's lap again and had fallen asleep. Jyn was stroking her hair. Alex was sitting on the floor between Lindsey's legs, and Morgan was in the huge, overstuffed chair in the other room having some tea. She seemed to want to be alone. She had a beautiful view of the woods outside. The sun was beginning to set and there were tears in her eyes. It would be the last Terran sunset she would see. But she would be sure that little Mandy would see many more of them, and that the world her granddaughter inherited would be better than she could ever hope for.

Jyn ached to comfort Morgan in the only way he knew how. He felt her loneliness and knew that she alone bore a responsibility that no one else on this world or his would ever understand. She was inconsolable but her resolve was strong. As he stroked Mandy's hair, he felt the love that she had for her granddaughter and her need to make earth a better place for her. She did not realize yet, that her sacrifice gave Mandy a dual inheritance. But he also knew that that knowledge would not ease Morgan's grief, or the grief she would feel as the memories of Earth left her the longer she stayed on Prymiah.

MORGAN THOUGHT WHAT Jyn could not realize that intertwined in the grief was anger. That hidden place that she kept from him by sheer will. She was still angry that her world was invaded. Still angry that her son must train to fight creatures able to kill him with one movement. And even though she loved Jyn, she hated that she wanted him. And she was no fool. She remembered the pain of the ravishments. Not the pleasurable pain that Jyn had given her. But the pain of her mind being bent to the will of another. The pain of struggling to keep this small part of her mind a secret. She could feel Jyn reaching for it, trying to invade it. Trying to ravish that part of her, just like he did the other parts. The -symbiote knew all of it, but could he somehow have kept it from Jyn? And yet, she knew he was using her too, he couldn't help it. He wanted to save his world as badly as Morgan wanted to save hers. So they worked in tandem. Soon, Jyn-Shaed would pierce this part of her too, and she would see how deep his love for her went.

'*It will still run deep, loved one.*'

And Morgan could feel Jyn-Shaed catching that last thought and holding on to it. Trying to glean what came before but unable to. She had already locked it tightly back into her mind for now. A piece of her that he couldn't access. She was thankful that the love she had for him covered the still simmering anger she carried for what was done to her and her world.

'*Not yet, my -Shaed. Let me hold on to this little piece of myself. Just a little longer.*'

AFTERWARD, MORGAN JOINED the others in the living room. It was time. Jyn said:

'Dr. Ren is coming over with our transport. She will be here soon.'

'Well, here it goes, then.' Alex said. Lindsey said:

'I need to clean the kitchen and dress Mandy for the trip.' Jyn said:

'That won't be necessary, besides, they are almost here, and Attendants will take care of your home while you're gone. Dr Ren will sedate you and I will put you in a dream state. The next time you awaken, you will be on board our vessel. Your bodies will need to adjust to the rhythm of our ship. It isn't like you would imagine space travel to be. Our engines mimic the rhythm of our world. It has a heartbeat.'

Lindsey seemed quite excited. She asked:

'Is it sentient?'

'Not in the way you imagine. But it is very responsive to us, and we are responsive to it. Your heart rates will slow down. If you were awakened too soon, it would be uncomfortable for you. Your blood will flow differently on our vessel. Your eyes must become acclimated to how we see on Prymiah. And your primal instincts-hunger, thirst, and yes, the desire to mate-will all be more intense.' Alex grunted and said:

'Great. All you people do is fuck and think about fucking.'

'You misunderstand, Alex.' Jyn said. 'On Prymiah, we don't have the same drive as you have seen us exhibit here. We mate far less than what you would think, but when we do, it's more intense. Our desire is more muted because we are home and are not driven by colonization. We work. We conduct business, we trade. Just like you do here. Our children go to school. We maintain our homes. You'll be surprised to see that Prymiah is not just one big bedroom.'

Jyn pushed Morgan and Lindsey to sleep lightly so he and Alex could speak freely. He needed Alex to know a few things before Dr. Ren arrived and she was close.

'Alex. Your mother doesn't think I know about the secret chamber in her mind. I knew the first time I was with her. She is a predator, and she is angry about what has happened to her and her world. She is angry about what has happened to her family. I would expect nothing less. She doesn't know that her anger is what fuels my passion to help her. To help you.'

'Why haven't you told her?'

'Because I want her to choose to tell me herself. I want her to love me enough to release that part of herself to me. It must be her choice. When she has finally told me, then I will know that she believes me. And I need her to trust me. Because when we arrive on Prymiah, I must tell her something she will not like.'

'Why are you telling me?'

'Because I need you to know the depth of my love for her. She may never release her thoughts to me. But I want you to know that I have full knowledge of what she will do for Earth and for her family, and I will not stop her. But there some things I must tell you man to man so that you will not be surprised when you awaken on my ship.'

'Oh no. Now what?'

'You will awaken in two weeks, then you will be able to move about freely. But we will keep little Mandy asleep for a few weeks after.'

'What for?'

'You will awaken full of desire for your wife. And all you will want to do for the first few days is mate.'

'What the?...'

'It's our pheromones. Mating is like eating on our world. It is a daily occurrence, and we are empathic. We feel each other's desires and even on races that are not naturally empathic, the remnants of our desire impact the minds of those we encounter. I'm telling you because as a male, you will want to be-enthusiastic-with Lindsey. She will desire you greatly, but you must be gentle-at least until you arrive on the planet, and she can be strengthened by it'.

'Sounds complicated. And messy.'

'You will get used to it. And it's not complicated. It's biology. But it can be messy. Remember, you were not influenced like your mom and dad. So, you will feel disoriented at times, like you are out of control. Compelled to mate. But for you it will be more disturbing because we will not interfere with the process. You'll adjust. You will find in time that adjusting will come quite easily for you.'

'What do you mean by that, Jyn?'

'It's time to transport. Dr Ren is here.'

This frightened Alex. He knew there were times he was too rough with Lindsey. He could feel her body resisting him, but she usually relented. He tried to do better by her. But he was embarrassed that he was too expressive in the bedroom. Lindsey was tough-that's why he loved her. And sometimes the drives he had seemed to overwhelm him.

But he knew he took advantage of her toughness. He was afraid that after what Jyn just told him, he would hurt her. Then he would be no better than that old tomcat.

CHAPTER TWO

MORGAN AWAKENED IN her and Jyn's assigned residence on the ship two weeks later. It was bigger than her house on earth. She wondered if she would ever get used to all this luxury. But for now, her main concern was how she felt. Everything had a shimmer to it-a glow. And she felt strange, like she would faint. She tried swinging her feet off the bed and went to stand, but before she could fall Jyn was at her side lifting her up. He smelled wonderful.

'Jyn, I think something is wrong with my eyes. Everything has a glow around it. You look-you look absolutely beautiful.'

'The atmosphere on our ship mimics the one on Prymiah. You will see like this for the rest of your life. We all look like we have auras around us. You, my loved one, look like a goddess. What else is different?'

'I feel like I am moving in slow motion. Almost like I could float to the ground. And there is a throbbing feeling against my skin. Inside too. Like a deep base that I can feel, but not hear.'

'Our planet's heartbeat. We had to keep you asleep until your body got used to it. When we travel to other worlds, it is this feeling I miss the most. The connection I have with my world. How does it make you feel?'

'Strange. And-

'And what, Morgan? Describe it. It pleases me to see you experience a portion of our world. Tell me what else you feel.'

'I'm extremely hungry. But I don't know what I crave. Every time I think of something that I liked on earth; I don't seem to want it. The taste I crave is some sort of sweetness. But I can't think of any fruit or convection on earth that mimics the flavor.'

'Stay here on the bed for just a little while. I'm going to bring you something to eat with a little water.'

Jyn came back with a small purple fruit. Morgan thought that it almost looked like an earth plum. He sat down next to her and cut it swiftly with his blade. The flesh inside was pale pink and it glistened. Not unlike Jyn's folds when he was aroused. Jyn captured her thought and smiled.

'It is curious that you would see the color of the flesh of this fruit and compare it to my arousal. Have a bite.'

When Morgan bit into it, it startled her. It was warm as if it had been warmed by the sun. It was extremely sweet, and as it went down her throat, she felt it all the way down into her stomach. Then she started to tingle all over, and she could feel herself becoming aroused.

'Jyn. What kind of fruit is this? We have nothing like it on earth.'

'It's a Guardian fruit. It is meant to be shared between lovers. Open your legs, I'll show you.'

Jyn was pleased to see that Morgan was already glistening with desire. She was even throbbing slightly to the rhythm of the ship, and he knew that would become more intense as she got closer to Prymiah. He took the other half of the fruit and rubbed it against her labia and her clitoris, slowly and deliberately until she came.

'Now look at the flesh of the fruit.'

'It's blue!'

'Taste it.'

'What? Jyn, I don't think I...'

'Trust me, Morgan. Taste it.'

Morgan took the fruit and tentatively bit into it. It was still sweet, but the flavor was markedly different, and it was cool going down her throat.

'Now, rub my folds.'

Morgan did as she was told, slowly rubbing the remaining fruit around Jyn's folds until she heard the familiar *pop*. Then Jyn gently took the fruit and bit into it. And when he did, the symbiote appeared from its resting place. Morgan noticed how the -seye glowed a soft and lovely blue and she could see his aura throbbing to the rhythm of the ship and when Jyn slipped into her, it was if all of her nerve endings felt every inch of him. It was intoxicating and they both came quickly. But Morgan found herself thoroughly satisfied and finally comfortable and at peace.

'Jyn. What *was* that?'

'Sometimes we don't have time to mate, but the desire is overwhelming. Our normal bonding times can be quite lengthy as you know. But the Guardian fruit helps us to reach orgasm quickly and the enzymes it contains has a small amount of sedative. Are you still hungry?'

'Not as much. I can wait.'

'Good. I have to speak with you about your consort, and that will give the Attendants time to prepare our meal.'

'Wait, Jyn. I thought there would be an audition, and that Varek and Elrek were the only contenders.'

'Things have changed. Varek has withdrawn.'

'How is that possible?'

'Because Elrek-seye convinced him that he is the better candidate. I agree.'

'Elrek-seye? Jyn. What is happening here? I mean really. How do you feel about that? Besides, Elrek has almost been like my *own* best friend. He has been my escort the whole time I was on earth when you weren't available. He has never been anything less than the perfect gentleman.'

'Elrek-seye has something to offer you that I cannot provide. He will be the perfect consort. I am forbidden to tell you why until you have bonded with him. I trusted him to guard you for a reason. He will come by after our meal to audition.'

'So soon? I haven't even been awake that long.'

'You are starting to sound like *earth* Morgan now. Not the Revered Mother.'

'Oh no. Isn't he the one who will be training Alex for combat?'

'Yes. It will enhance Alex's training, because Alex will want to kill him.'

WHEN THE DOOR CHIME sounded, Morgan jumped out of her skin. Jyn just chuckled. He knew this was uncomfortable for her. He wondered if she would ever get used to Prymiahn ways. Morgan didn't know what to expect. She was still disoriented from waking. But this was sobering her up quick. Jyn answered the door.

'Revered Mother, it would be my honor to serve as your consort. Please allow me to show you what I have to offer.'

Morgan stood almost dumfounded at Elrek-seye's rugged beauty. He was dressed in his battle regalia. Where Jyn looked like a prince, Elrek looked like a warrior. He was bigger and taller than Jyn. His hair was tied in a ponytail, but it draped past his back. His hands were huge, but his fingers long and slender. Jyn, curiously, did not hiss.

Jyn said:

'Enter and prove yourself to my wife.'

Jyn then led them both to a small chair that was only big enough for two to sit very closely together. Morgan felt heat coming from Elrek-seye and it made her uncomfortable. Jyn left the room and closed the door gently behind him. Elrek-seye turned to her and looked her deeply in the eyes. His aura was soft and white, and he looked like what she imagined her Guardian angel would look. He smiled.

'Revered Mother, I am no angel. But I am here to show you what I can be to you as your consort. Please take my hand and allow me to show you a vision.'

Morgan took Jyn's hands and was surprised at how soft they were, but he held her strongly and in that strength, she felt tenderness. Elrek did not show her a vision of his -seye, nor did she see anything sexual at all. But what he showed her shocked her more than anything she could have been shown.

Elrek-seye showed every moment he had seen her, from the time he scouted her the first time on earth, until this moment. He showed her how he felt when he laid eyes on her. The longing he had for her. Not just sexual longing. But a longing to know her as his own. She saw herself through his eyes. And in his eyes, she was beautiful. As the vision ended, she found his lips on hers, and he kissed her lovingly and deeply-even more than Bruce-but that kiss was so needed and so full of promise that she felt herself needing him and wanting him. But as she began to lean into him, he released her.

At that moment, Jyn walked in. He saw his best friend, glowing and flushed like he was on the evening of his Vrek-mal with his wife Kiisma-seae. And he saw Morgan, blushing and breathless. She was full of desire and curiosity. He loved them both. He said:

'Loved one, do you accept Elrek-seye as your consort, to satisfy your need at your behest?'

'Yes, my -Shaed, I accept Elrek-seye to serve as my consort.'

Jyn said:

'As is the tradition of our people, Elrek-seye, I release my wife, the Revered Mother, to you for her enjoyment starting tomorrow and until her needs are met. And I pledge to not bond with her until you have fulfilled your duty. But if you displease her, it will certainly mean your death. Do you understand?'

'Yes, my -Shaed. I understand. Revered Mother, my precious one, I will return tomorrow, to escort you to my bed. It is my hope that I will meet your need, but pledge that if I don't, I will reveal my neck to the blade of Jyn-Shaed.'

'I will be ready, Elrek-seye.'

But Morgan was more than ready. She found herself unexpectedly aching and longing for Elrek.

As Jyn escorted Elrek outside, he said to him:

'Elrek. I am honored. But I know you. I know what you have waiting for her.'

'Jyn. You also know I am quite skilled. She will not be harmed. Remember. My wife felt no pain at our Vrek-mal.'

'Your wife was Prymiahn.'

'And the Revered Mother is more Prymiahn than Terran. When I have fulfilled her need, she will be even closer.'

'Do you know what her need is?'

Elrek-seye smiled, and Jyn knew that that question was one that was not for him to know. He knew that when Morgan left in the morning, she would return to him changed. Then the two men embraced warmly and parted ways. When Jyn went inside, he found Morgan standing and looking quite dumfounded. And beautiful. But he couldn't touch her. He would be sleeping in a separate bed. It was going to be long night.

BEFORE THE AUDITION, Elrek-seye had a conversation with his wife.

Elrek-seye was frustrated. Kiisma knew it. He was constantly pacing the floor.

'Elrek-seye. Stop it. When are you going to tell Jyn and Morgan how you feel? They already know. This is ridiculous.'

'I know they know. But I still feel like I'm betraying Jyn somehow.'

'Elrek. You saved him. In more ways than one. You are closer to him than any other. He loves you. You have suffered more than most on this world. Remember, I am your loved one. I know.'

'Yes. And what about you, Kiisma? How do you feel?'

'Elrek. Why do you ask me what you already know? I could not be happier that you wish to pursue the Revered Mother. It would only serve to enhance our relationship. Kilra said she is quite wonderful to be around. She is fiercely protective of her planet and would kill for it. But she loves our world, too. And from what I am told, she is very open to our ways. But you know all of this. And you said that you have made a connection with her. What is it really? You are hiding a part of your mind from me. You know there is no shame between us.'

Elrek remembered a moment he had with Morgan while still on earth.

Morgan had gotten accustomed to traveling around the huge compound with Elrek. She liked him a great deal. He was an enigma to her. She knew he was serious about protecting her. And because he was so tall and muscular she felt exceptionally safe. She felt him bristle when other Prymiahns let their curiosity get the best of them and got too close. But he never hissed. One stern look from him was all they needed, then it was a polite 'Good morning, Revered Mother' and they were quickly on their way.

At first, she was uncomfortable. She still didn't see herself as royalty. But Elrek made her feel at ease to the point of feeling that she was just doing some errands with a close friend. He also had a very dry sense of humor, and unlike Jyn-Shaed, he didn't make her feel emotionally naked.

One day she wanted to go to the market to find some cooking utensils to make Jyn's favorite dish. She was finally learning how to cook in the way he was accustomed and decided to give up trying to do it with Terran equipment. They had Attendants to handle the cooking of course, but Morgan wanted to know how. Elrek seemed to enjoy her curiosity about his culture, and they shared a laugh or two about how unfamiliar it all was to her.

She accidentally slipped and fell backward into his substantial chest. He grabbed her firmly at her shoulders then relaxed and held her close to him. They both remained in that position for just a moment.

'Elrek. Thank you.'

Elrek remained silent. But his thoughts were unguarded for just a moment. Then he said:

'I'm sorry. Please forgive me.'

'There's nothing to forgive, Elrek. I consider you a friend. And more than that, I...'

'Please don't speak of it.'

And Morgan didn't. They continued their errands, and after resting their tender thoughts, began to laugh and enjoy the day again.

Close to the end of their shopping trip, Morgan allowed her thoughts to wander back to the moment Elrek held her. She felt herself flush and allowed her mind to imagine what it would be like to be with him. Then she realized he was not next to her. She stopped and looked behind her, and he was standing with his hand outstretched. He said:

'I have something I want to give you.'

Morgan caught his hand and immediately had a vision of him kissing her softly on the lips. She could feel the velvety softness of his skin and how warm he was. She felt his breath begin to quicken, and just as she began to submit to his kiss fully, he released his hand.

And because she understood what was between them, she remained silent and allowed their eyes to meet and agree to the secret although they both knew that Jyn-Shaed would know the moment he saw either of them.

They also knew that Jyn would no doubt approve. So they shared a smile and Elrek escorted Morgan home.

After resting on that memory, he continued the conversation with his wife.

'I am afraid that I...'

'Will cause her pain. I know more than most where this fear comes from. Your -seye has been especially swollen lately, but I have enjoyed you with no pain whatsoever. You know that. What has Jyn told you of his experience with her?'

'That she is quite insatiable. Open to his advances. And very creative. He said she has opened his eyes to greater pleasures.'

'So why do you hesitate? You are an Alpha. Just like Jyn. More so in my opinion. You also know that I have enjoyed Jyn before, so I will not lack the comfort of a lover if you are her consort.'

'Yes. That gives me some comfort.'

'Let me speak with her. I'll give her a woman's view. I hear she is quite principled. Her hesitation will only come from her own lingering Terran morals.'

KIISMA MET WITH MORGAN in the same café that Bruce met with Jyn. It was a lovely day, and Morgan was looking forward to meeting Elrek's wife. He had been so kind to her.

'Revered Mother, it is an honor to have lunch with you today.'

'Would you just call me Morgan? I feel I know you already, through Elrek. And I really need friends. Not followers.' Kiisma smiled.

'Well, Morgan. Thank you. I'll get to it then. My husband desires to be your consort but is hesitant to apply.'

Morgan blushed. She should be used the direct conversations of the Prymiahns by now, but sometimes they still shocked her. She said:

'Well. I was not expecting our conversation to start out quite so abruptly, but that is your way, I suppose.'

'Yes. But more to the point. I think I know why Elrek is hesitant.'

'I would be less than honest if I told you I was not attracted to him. But I myself am hesitant to intrude into the relationship he has with you.'

'But you know our ways are more liberal in matters of love and sex.'

'Yes. I am trying to become accustomed to it.'

'Do you love Jyn and Bruce? Not in the same ways of course, but equally?'

'Yes. I found that fact to be a lovely aspect of your culture. The giving and receiving of love seems boundless for Prymiahns.'

'Do you feel that you could love Elrek? Just as equally? Even if it is not in the same way?'

'Yes. I do feel that way. My thoughts have been resting on him quite frequently.'

'Well that's good. I was hoping so, although I suspected it already. Your heart has been racing since my arrival. I know it's not me. It's thoughts of him that you are trying to suppress. Please allow them to be free. They excite me as well.'

'You are indeed a strange and wonderful race, Kiisma. But my feelings are not what brings you here.'

'You are quite perceptive. No. My reasons are to find why my husband is so hesitant to express his feelings to you openly. I think I see. You are unique to us. A rare jewel. He does not want to disappoint you.'

'Elrek has been nothing but kind to me. A true gentleman. He could not disappoint me.'

'Elrek has a ... unique characteristic. He is afraid you will be taken aback.'

'Kiisma. I've seen and experienced quite a lot in my time on Earth. What could it possibly be?'

'His -seye. It is an ancient Alpha. Older than Jyn's. And it is quite large.'

'I see. I also see you sitting in front of me. You look like you are in one piece. You are beautiful. You have many children by him. You love him greatly because you are here to advocate for him. You are dressed in the finest of Prymiahn clothing and he has covered you with precious metals and jewels from your world. You are obviously his loved one. His first. And you will remain his first love long after I am dead.'

Kiisma took a deep breath. She understood why Morgan of Earth was the Revered Mother. And why her husband had fallen to love her. She wanted nothing more than her husband to have his need fulfilled by her. She said:

'You honor me by your words, Morgan of Earth. Elrek's love for you is well placed. Shall I tell him to proceed?'

'Yes, Kiisma.'

'He probably will not speak of it until the time comes. He holds his feelings close to his heart until he feels free to release them.'

'I assumed that of him. The strong and silent type, huh?'

'Yes. That's Elrek.'

They both smiled at this. And continued their lunch. When Kiisma returned home from lunch, Elrek was pacing the floor again.

'Oh Elrek. Stop it already. Your feelings are well placed. She will not reject you. In fact. I think she has a great desire for you. You will have no problem giving of yourself. And she will have no problem receiving you.' Elrek said:

'How can that be, Kiisma? She does not possess a -seae'

'While I was with her, I sensed her hunger for you. She is already preparing for you in her mind. She does not know it yet, but she is. And I was drawn to her as well. She is wonderful to be around, just like you said. So that settles it. Come, let's enjoy each other. Put your mind at rest.'

CHAPTER THREE

BEFORE THEY LEFT EARTH, Elrek also had a meeting with Varek.

'Thank you for meeting me, Varek. I have a request you will not like.'

'What is it?'

'I want you to withdraw your audition to be the Revered Mother's consort.'

'Why would I do that? You know my desire for her. But now that I see you, I understand.'

'Not fully.'

'Why do you say that?'

'I was outside of their residence the night he...'

'The night of the Vrek-mal?'

'No. The second time he ravished her. The Bond of Duty Ritual. I felt her misery, her pain.'

'Elrek. She accepted him back into her bed. It was verified by Idra and Dr. Ren.'

'I know that Varek. I have also been with her from the beginning. Even before Jyn-seye. I have seen all her desires. Ones she had before she became the Revered Mother.'

'Elrek. What are you straining against?'

'I wanted to kill your brother for causing her pain. I wanted to kill Jyn. He is my closest ally, but for him to expose her to his first was vulgar and cruel. He did it only for his benefit. He should have died the day he killed that poor girl, but you stayed my hand.'

'The Revered Mother believes him to be redeemed and has forgiven him. She loves him.'

'I know this Varek. But I need her. I need her to see that love is not always pain. She had more than enough of that on earth.'

'You are in love with her.'

'Yes.'

'You know she will not be your wife. Your purpose is only to serve her the desire her husbands cannot.'

'I know this, Varek! Why are you questioning me? Besides, we don't know what the future holds.'

'Elrek. I love you as much as I love my own brother. I see you are aching for her. I also know your power. You are more of an Alpha than most of us. You have suffered more than most of us because of it. But you have turned your suffering into a great passion. I am the High Priest. It is my duty to make sure you understand the consequences of what you ask.'

'I do. But I cannot audition against you. I also love you as a brother. And I know the gifts you would bring to her. But yes, my power is great, and my ache is unbearable. The gift I will give her will soothe her pain.'

'How does your wife feel about all of this? I assume I know. But tell me if I am right.'

'Kiisma yearns for me to have her. In my desire, I have spent my passion on her. She enjoys it, but she is tired, Varek. She has already had one child within the time we have been on earth and is pregnant again.'

'Elrek. You have seven children now. Your virility will gain you a permanent seat on the council if you keep this up, and I know you hate politics.'

'I cannot contain the seed of my -seye.'

'It is forbidden for a consort to impregnate the Revered Mother. Only her Prymiahn husband may have that honor.'

'You know a way to keep me from being fertile. At least for now.'

'Yes. As High Priest, I can provide a plant extract that will suppress your 'seyes ability to produce seed, but there are side effects, and you won't like them.'

'What side effects?'

'Everything on Prymiah is balance, you know this.'

'Yes.'

'If a 'seye is prevented from producing seed, it's fluid will increase in volume. You will swell with misery until it releases itself.'

'I see.'

'Yes. And we both know how you suffered during your revelation. It will be as if you are reliving that moment again. And you must consume the extract each time you are to be with her. If you forget, you will impregnate her, and there will be a scandal.'

'What happens if I do?'

'You must then fight your best friend to the death for the right to be her -Shaed. And from the look in your eyes I see that you are willing to do that. I will not withdraw my audition unless you promise me that you will not impregnate Morgan. I know you would kill Jyn, and flawed or not Elrek, he is my brother. Pledge that to me and I will withdraw my audition. Although it pains me to do so. I was so hoping to have her in my bed.'

Elrek hissed loudly.

'Calm down, Elrek. I see your love for her. Be careful. Do you pledge that you will refrain from releasing your fertile seed into her?'

'I pledge it, Varek. For now.'

'Then I withdraw my audition in your favor. Now let me show you how to consume the extract. I'm going to give you more than you need for the Revered Mother. You may consider taking it when you are with your wife. Poor Kiisma. You should be ashamed. And I have caught your thoughts. I pray to the goddess that your heart is finally fulfilled.'

They both chuckled at this, but Elrek was already aroused in anticipation, and Varek was worried.

'I ALMOST FORGOT, LOVED one, Elrek has left you a gift. He instructed me to give it to you after your acceptance of him.'

'Oh?'

'Yes. He was quite insistent. And he left instructions.'

Morgan already had a pit in her stomach. She couldn't relax. She almost fell into the chair and her hands were shaking as she unwrapped it. Jyn looked at her with amused curiosity.

When she opened, it she gasped. It was a sheer gown. It seemed to be made of pure light. Golden threads shimmered within the fabric. It had long sleeves and was opened at the neck. She had never seen anything like it on earth.

'Jyn. Is this really glowing? Or is it my eyes again?'

'It's both. The thread is from a plant that only grows deep in our ocean. It glows only when exposed to the air. The glow will never dissipate. And your eyes are seeing how it looks on Prymiah. On earth, I don't know how it would look to you. I would imagine it would be just as beautiful. More so with you inside of it. It is quite exquisite. And very expensive. It is a gift only a lover would give.'

'Jyn. This is too much. What is happening here, really? I never imagined this from him.'

'But you accepted him. Why?'

'I am comfortable with him. I knew taking a consort was a requirement of my position. I was relieved when I found out Elrek was auditioning. I believe I can trust him.'

'You will do more than trust him, loved one. He auditioned because he desires you.'

'I know. And I *am* curious. I just don't understand all of these rituals and partnerships. It seems so promiscuous.'

'That's Earth whispering in your ear. Remember, we have no such inhibitions here. It's biology, and pleasure is part of that.'

'Aren't you...'

'Jealous? Angry? Not at all. My only concern is your happiness. Your pleasure. You believe you have experienced everything because of your age. Remember, we live hundreds of years. We are still discovering the depths of pleasure. We relish in it. Elrek has something you desire. Something you crave.'

'How could he possibly know?'

'Morgan, some things are meant to be between you and him. I must leave it at that.'

'I see. What are the other instructions?'

'I will bathe you before he arrives. I will dress you in the gown. You will wear nothing underneath it. But I will put you in a covering so he may escort you safely to quarters that have been designated for you both.' He will present his intention to me, and I will release you to him. Next time you require his company, you may request him on your own. But he must not request you. No matter how much he desires you, he must wait until you summon him.'

'What if I never want to see him again?'

'Then you won't. But loved one, you will crave him. And of this, you can be certain.'

CHAPTER FOUR

JYN FINISHED BATHING Morgan and dried her off. Morgan was amazed at how gentle he was. And how quiet. She let him be. He seemed to be pensive. Not quite present. But she sensed no apprehension in him. She smelled him though, his pheromones were strong but not overpowering. But she was surprised at catching his scent. It seemed that lately she found it easier. He slipped the dress Elrek gave her over her head. Everywhere it touched her skin, it caused a sensation.

'Jyn! What's happening? Everywhere the fabric touches, my skin tingles!'

Jyn smiled at his wife. He could see her nipples hardening through the sheerness of the dress.

'It's the enzymes on the fabric. It is meant to do that. That is why it is a gift between lovers. Here, let me cover you with your ceremonial robe. Elrek is almost here.'

At that moment, the chime sounded.

'Stand just behind me, loved one.'

Morgan did as she was asked.

Jyn opened the door. Morgan gasped at the sight of Elrek. He was dressed for battle again, but his hair was loosened from the ponytail and covered his shoulders like a white mantle. He was stunning. Morgan had never seen him like this.

'My -Shaed. I have come to pleasure your wife. Will you release her to me?'

'She is released.'

Jyn then took Morgan's trembling hand and placed it on Elrek's forearm. Then like a gentleman, he bowed at Jyn-Shaed, and they left, walking slowly to their meeting place.

Morgan was too breathless to speak, and the fabric was rubbing deliciously over her nipples. Elrek was walking purposefully and slowly, so they would have time to speak. He said:

'Precious one. Why are you so uncertain?'

'Elrek, I have known you for so long as a dear friend. But I find that I am losing myself in your presence. It bothers me because I can't explain it.'

'No Morgan. It bothers you because you can't control it. Desire is not forbidden on Prymiah. You are still bound to Earth. But you are so much more than you realize. I want you to try speaking to me without moving your mouth. And I want you to try to feel my thoughts. You have been around us for quite a while, and I know that you have become more sensitive. You are even beginning to catch our pheromones now. If we can speak telepathically, you will be more comfortable expressing yourself as we are intimate.'

This caused Morgan to blush.

'Try to feel my thoughts, Morgan. Just relax and allow your mind to focus on me.' He began:

'How do you like my gift?'

'I only get a glimpse, of what you said, Elrek. I could only catch 'gift'.'

Elrek moved his left hand up from her waist so he could lightly rub her hardened nipple. This caught Morgan by surprise, and she let out an 'Oh!' Elrek did not stop but continued to rub it lightly.

'How do you like my gift?'

'It's lovely, it makes me tingle all over. Wait! I can hear you!'

'Because you are focused on me. When I aroused your nipple, it caused your mind to focus on my thoughts because you want to be close to me. Is that true?'

'Yes. Oh yes. Right now I want you inside of me. Oh. I'm sorry.'

'Why are you sorry? I can tell you are trying to block me. Stop. You shouldn't be ashamed.'

'Yes I should. I'm still uncomfortable at times, even after everything I've done. Sometimes, I think that I have lost my mind and given myself over to the vulgar.'

'It is not vulgar, Morgan. It's primal. On our world it is expected that we allow our primal selves to take control on occasion. I have found that when I do, I am able to experience the greatest pleasure. This is why I wanted you to speak to me telepathically. You can express your primal self to me alone without embarrassment.'

'I don't know if I can.'

'You will precious one. You won't be able to control it. We are here.'

Elrek opened the door to a luxurious space. A large bed framed inside an enclosure with no walls, but sheer draperies around it. To the left a large bathing area with a toilet room that was closed off for privacy. To the rear, an eating area. And in the front a seating area with several large chairs that looked perfectly comfortable for activities that did not include much sitting. Elrek closed the door and gently took off Morgan's robe, revealing her nakedness underneath the dress he had given her. He left the dress on her, but lifted her and carried her to the bed, gently laying her on it. Morgan gasped.

'Elrek? Are we going to jump right in? Right now?'

'Morgan, I am not your husbands. My purpose is to give you what you need. First, I must find what that is, and I am eager to start. I have loved you from the moment I saw you. And I have longed for you.'

He positioned himself next to her but did not take off his clothing.

'You aren't undressing?'

'I don't need them off to pleasure you. You will see more of me than you expect, I imagine. But I will take my time.'

Elrek started rubbing her nipples gently, causing Morgan to groan. Then he grasped one of them between his fingers. He didn't pinch but closed his fingers slightly and rubbed the nipple firmly between them. Because her dress was still on, the fabric caused even more sensations to her delicate skin.

'I see you like this. You are blushing, and your breathing is getting faster.'

'Elrek-I...I don't think I can stand this.'

'You have leaned into the pain all of your life. Now you must learn to lean into the pleasure. Let it happen to you. Open your legs for me. I will never force you.'

Morgan opened her legs, and Elrek slid her dress up slowly above her waist making sure the fabric rubbed against her legs. Then he began to manipulate the rings on her clitoris.

'Umm, Morgan, you are already aroused. I wonder how you will taste. Slow your breathing. Lean into the feeling. Shall I add another finger?'

'Y-yes, oh yes, Elrek! Then fuck me, please fuck me!'

'Not yet, precious one. You are not nearly ready. Let me help you.'

Elrek kept fingering Morgan until she started to wiggle. He breathed down her neck, causing her to tremble. She was about to cum, and he stopped suddenly.

'Elrek! Please don't stop. I almost came!'

'I know. But I don't want you to yet.'

Elrek then stood up and slowly began removing his clothing. He was incredibly slow and watched Morgan closely the entire time. Morgan saw the ruggedness of his chest and the scars of battle. She saw that he was glistening with sweat. When he removed his pants she was surprised that his -seye was not visible. But his folds were extremely swollen-like Jyn's was when she taught him to masturbate. He lay next to her again and began rubbing her nipples like before.

'*You look for my -seye, but he will show himself when you are ready. My symbiote and I are a lot closer than most. We work completely in tandem and have from my revelation, so he knows my timing and I know his.*'

He then gently rolled nearly on top of Morgan but did not rest his weight on her. He leaned to one side on his elbow and draped his left leg over her legs. Her desire was great, and this pleased him. Heat was radiating from him.

'*Morgan, I need you to look deeply into my eyes. I want to show you a vision. I will speak to you through it. I need you to speak back with no shame.*'

Morgan did as she was told and as she looked into Elrek's eyes it was if she was transported into another time and space. She was an observer looking on at something that was about to take place.

'*Morgan, what do you see?*'

'*A lovely garden, it's dark outside but the moons are out. I see a Prymiah woman. She is naked.*'

'*That is my wife, Kiisma.*'

'*She is beautiful. Her hair is loosened like yours is right now. She appears to be looking for someone.*'

'*She is looking for me. It is our Vrek-mal.*'

'*Elrek. This is...intimate.*'

'*I know. But you want to see, don't you?*'

'*Yes.*'

Elrek easily slid his fingers inside of her again. She was so wet. Her arousal was growing.

'*Tell me why you want to see. Don't be ashamed. Tell me.*'

'*I want to see you take her.*'

'*You want to see me fuck her.*'

'*Yes.*'

'*Why?*'

'*I don't know.*'

'*Keep watching and we'll find out. Here I come. Now what do you see?*'

'She's not running, like most Prymiahn women do. She is walking away from you slowly. Swinging her hips. She is teasing you! She wants you to catch her!'

'Yes. Does she look afraid?'

'No. She looks... hungry. She's holding her hand out behind her.'

'Yes. Do you see my -seye?'

'Not yet.'

'Oh Morgan, you are so wet, you are opening up. I have all of my fingers inside of you. Why are you so aroused? Tell me.'

'I want to see you inside of her. I want to see the look on her face as she submits to you. I want you to cum inside of her and I want to see it.'

Morgan started moving against his fingers until his whole fist was inside of her. His hand was completely soaked.

'Lean into the pleasure Morgan, I will not allow you to release yet. Now what do you see?'

'You have caught her by the hand, and she turns to face you. You kiss her lightly on the mouth. She is getting on her knees to expose herself to you. Oh!'

'Do you see my -seye?'

'Y-yes. Elrek. It is. Huge.'

'I feel your breath quickening, Morgan. Are you frightened?'

'A little. But...'

'You want to keep watching.'

'Yes.'

Elrek had slowly released his wet fist from Morgan. She remained wet and open.

'Keep watching. Tell me what's happening.'

'You are entering her. You are slowly sliding in. You are impossibly sliding all the way in!'

'What does Kiisma's face tell you?'

'She looks relieved, but she also looks frustrated. She is getting down on her elbows. She wants you to...thrust harder.'

'Yes. Keep watching and tell me what you see now.'

'You are beginning to thrust slowly inside of her.'

'Ahh, yes Morgan. I've waited so long.'

'Oh Elrek! I feel you inside of me!'

'Yes, precious one. I am as deep and comfortable inside of you as I was with Kiisma on the night of our Vrek-mal. Keep watching and tell me how you feel.'

'Her face is full of ecstasy. Elrek, I can't... I can't hold back. Please let me cum! You feel so good inside of me!'

'Not yet. Watch. You must watch until the end. Tell me what is happening now.'

'You are moving faster. She is...screaming. But not from pain. She is screaming from ecstasy. Is that possible? Elrek, you are thrusting stronger. More slowly, but stronger. Oh Elrek! You feel so good. What is happening to me?'

'That is the beginning of your release. What do you see now?'

'You have released yourself inside of her. You are slowly pulling out and your seed is falling out of her as you do. Elrek!'

And Elrek allowed Morgan to finally cum and when she did, she screamed louder than she ever did with Jyn-Shaed. And just as she had seen in the vision, Elrek slowly pulled out of her and as he did, his desire flowed from inside of her and still his -seye convulsed liquid as he allowed his -seye to lay itself on Morgan's chest while it continued to release itself.

'Let your eyes rest on what has given you so much pleasure, Morgan.'

Morgan looked down at the huge member laying heavily and wet across her chest. It was beautiful and lethal. With a large mouth and canines almost as big as Jyn's. It was still throbbing liquid from itself. The fluid was warm and hot and inviting. She stroked it along its length, and it welcomed her touch by lengthening and shortening itself between her breasts deliciously like a fat snake. She then placed her fingers to her lips to taste the symbiote's fluid and it was extremely sweet but spicy. Like the taste of cinnamon had caressed her tongue. But she was amazed because Elrek's -seye simply looked like it would have never fit.

'Elrek. How?'

'When a female is truly aroused and the male is completely focused on her pleasure, she expands to accommodate him. Size is usually of no consequence if the woman is sufficiently prepared.

'I am still throbbing. Like he is still inside of me.'

'You desire him again?'

'Yes.'

'Good. But I must have you wait. There are more pleasures I want to show you.'

'Does he bite?'

'Yes. But it does not hurt. It feels-different.'

'Elrek. I still ache for you to be inside of me.'

'Good.'

'What do you mean?'

'I am experienced in pleasure torture, precious one. I am meant to bring you to ecstasy. That does not happen quickly.'

'But. Aren't you miserable during? Don't you suffer?'

'Yes. And I have suffered for over two years, hoping to be inside of you. I intend for you to ache for me so I can show you everything you have missed as a woman.'

'Is that how you captured Kiisma?'

'Yes. Even during Vrek-mal, she has never felt pain from me. But she has been driven almost mad with ecstasy. Now it is time for us to bathe. I will draw you a bath and join you after I have changed the bed. It is quite wet.'

'I'm afraid your gift is ruined.'

'Not at all. It cleans quite easily. And for the rest of the evening, you will not need clothes.'

Morgan was amazed at how quickly Elrek drew a bath. She slipped out of her dress and stepped inside. It felt so good to be enveloped in the warmth of the water. She could hear him changing the bed and was beginning to drift off to sleep when she felt his presence. She was tired, so she decided to speak to him normally. She saw that his -seye had not retreated and continued to be slightly erect. She still wondered to herself how it could have possibly fit inside of her. Of course Elrek heard this thought and smiled.

'Do you mind if I join you? You look absolutely beautiful, and I want to show you something.'

'Please.'

Elrek slipped in the generous bathtub with Morgan and straddled her legs. Then he kissed her fully and deeply. He groaned along her neck. She felt herself opening up again and Elrek's fingers found her clit.

'You are insatiable, Morgan. I will fulfill your need. Look at my tongue.'

Morgan could see tiny spines on it. Just like a cat's tongue.

'Why didn't I feel those when you kissed me?'

'I control them.'

He then grasped her right breast and licked it gently, letting the spines brush against it. He felt her tremble, then he did the other.

'Tell me how that feels, Morgan.'

'Oh. Elrek. It. It feels so good.'

Elrek stopped. Morgan could still feel the sensation on her nipples. And she was still throbbing on the inside.

'Talk to me Morgan. Tell me what's happening.'

'Elrek you know what's happening.'

'You are still resisting your primal self. Stop it.'

'I want to...'

'You want to what?'

'I want to have you again. I want you to fill me up again and again. I don't ever want to be without you inside of me. I want you to lick my pussy with your rough tongue and then I want you to fuck me.'

Elrek got out of the tub and helped Morgan out. She noticed his -seye was starting to swell even more and it excited her. Elrek gently dried her off and then himself and led her back to the bed.

'Lay on your stomach, Morgan.'

When she did, he took his rough tongue and slowly licked her from her lower back to the base of her scalp. He took his time. His tongue was so warm. She started to moan.

'Turn over and open your legs wide.'

'Elrek don't.'

'Why not? Are you afraid? You told me what you desire, and I intend to fulfill your need.'

'Yes. I'm still afraid, Elrek. Of losing control. I already feel like I'm going to explode.'

Elrek began licking around her labia. She started to whimper.

'Lean into the pleasure, Morgan. Feel it. Explode. I'll drink it all.'

He began licking her clit and then darting his tongue just inside of her. She felt the heat of his breath. Then she started to move with his tongue. She was just about to come when Elrek stopped and gently pushed his -seye all the way into her, wetly and deeply, and then he began to groan and thrust hard.

'Elrek, I am going to die. You are going to kill me.'

'I will take you to the gates of death to pleasure you my precious one.'

Then he slowed his thrusts to a stop and let his -seye take control, causing Morgan to squirt profusely. And as Elrek slowly pulled out of her he bent down to her pussy and licked her firmly until she came again in his mouth.

Later, once he had finally allowed Morgan to rest, he revealed to her what her desire is.

'You like to watch. You are a voyeur. You enjoy the primal act and like to see every aspect of it. When I was showing you the vision of my Vrek-mal with Kiisma, you watched intently. I felt your arousal. You were most aroused at my penetration of her, and her reaction to it. That was when I finally penetrated you. You were so wet, Morgan. So open and ready. You feel more connected sexually when you observe others mating. This is truly Prymiahn, and it amazes me. When we are together, I can show you visions of different conquests with females of different worlds if you like. Most never experience any pain, but each has their own way of expressing the primal. It will be very stimulating for you, and very intimate for me. Would you like that?'

'Yes, Elrek. I would.'

'Good. Get a good night's rest. Tomorrow, I will live inside of you.'

AS ELREK WAS ESCORTING Morgan back to Jyn-Shaed the next evening, she was very quiet. Elrek said:

'Why are you so quiet? You don't need to speak it, just send your thoughts to me like you did before.'

'How will it be with Jyn? He's not as... substantial as you are.'

'It will be better now. You will see. It will surprise you. Our DNA was infused with your own and it has special properties. There is no need for concern in that area.'

'I'm still feeling a need.'

'I know. It is my way. I want you to need me. Soon, that feeling will fade, but only fade. I intend for you to always feel me inside of you.'

'Why, Elrek?'

'Because I'm your lover. And I know that you understand a part of yourself that you didn't before, and I also know that if left to your own choice you would

deny yourself with the mistaken belief that to allow yourself pleasure, you would be acting selfishly. Will you deny I'm speaking the truth?'

'No.'

'But don't worry. It will not be a constant feeling. But when you need a release that only I can give you, you will know. And you will summon me. I will be with you in a moment of time. 'We are almost there. Is there anything you need to tell me before I return you to your husband?'

'I am afraid of how I feel.'

'I know.'

Jyn was waiting at their entrance as Elrek and Morgan arrived. He was dressed for battle and his blade was drawn. He looked lethal and lovely, and Morgan's heart melted.

'Elrek-seye, I see you are returning my wife to me. Morgan of Earth, Revered Mother of Prymiah, did Elrek-seye bring you the pleasure you required?'

'Yes, my -Shaed, Elrek-seye satisfied my need.'

'Are you ready to return to me?'

'Yes, my -Shaed, I am ready to return to you.'

Jyn returned his blade to its sheath.

'Elrek-seye, you may release my wife to me, and as you have fulfilled your duty as her consort, I release you to be summoned by her at her request and will not deny you as a member of my family.'

'Thank you, my -Shaed.'

And as Elrek left he sent Morgan a deliciously subtle thought, which aroused her, and pleased Jyn-Shaed.

CHAPTER FIVE

JYN WAS PLEASED TO see Morgan, even though it had only been two days. He had missed her. But he wanted to simply speak to her for a while. Getting her to bed was a given, of course. But he needed her conversation. He had poured wine for them both and invited her to sit and relax.

'How did you enjoy your visit with Elrek? I mean, I don't need the intimate details. But I would like to know your impression of him? He is my second in command, after all.'

Morgan was glad to talk about it. She had so many questions. Elrek seemed so mysterious and serious about lovemaking. He was almost *too* intense. Jyn smiled at that thought. He said:

'Yes. Elrek is very intense. He is that way in everything that he does. But the way he is when he is intimate, I think that has a lot to do with his revelation and what took place after.'

'Tell me.'

'Elrek suffered a lot longer with his symbiote. Most young men have their revelations when they are about 13 or so. My own happened late too. I was 15. But Elrek was 17 when he had his. He was almost at the end of his junior studies, and he was planning to go to the military academy afterward. But men cannot join the academy until after their revelations, So Elrek was getting more and more anxious every day. Not to mention his discomfort. His folds stayed swollen relentlessly, and they were huge. He always felt them. You and Idra have told me how uncomfortable it is when your breast milk comes in. Your breasts begin to feel as though they aren't yours. That they are just hindrances until the babies can finally suckle, then the feeling changes. I can't describe the pain properly. But it wasn't just pain. It was arousal. Elrek was constantly aroused. Even rubbing the folds didn't give him much relief. To function in school he had to bind the folds. By the time he got home from class, the binding material was soaked. I can't imagine his suffering. As close as we were even then, he never complained. But I could feel his agony.

'He still made the best grades in our class. And the girls were naturally curious. Our revelations are always public, and he got a lot of teasing from the boys. One day we were all sitting in class like normal. Elrek was in particularly good spirits and all of a sudden he started to scream for me to take off his bindings. I'll never forget how miserable he sounded. Like a wounded animal. I lifted his shirt to lower his pants slightly, and unwrapped him as fast as I could, and I could already see blood. He started shrieking and tears were running down his face. He kept saying '*It's eating me, Jyn!*' over and over.

'I was the closest to him. The other kids backed away, but they kept looking-you know because they were curious. The first thing I saw in the center of the folds was the symbiote's teeth. And the canines. They were already as large as mine are now. And when the head emerged it was fully developed. His symbiote ripped past his folds and pulled itself and its swollen scrotum completely out of Elrek. He was screaming the whole time, and when it was finally out, it became completely filled with seed, fully erect, and ejaculated all over Elrek, me, and most of the class. Elrek then passed out.'

'Oh my God, Jyn. I can't imagine.'

'I can still hear him screaming and smell the blood. The boys, believe it or not were ecstatic. It was the biggest they had ever seen. But the girls, they looked scared. I had another classmate help me carry Elrek to the recovery center. He was there for a couple of days. It took one of those days just for the symbiote to shrink down and retreat into its folds. Elrek tells me it never completely shrinks. His parents decided it would be best to let him recover at home for a couple of weeks, but it was during that time he revealed the girl he wanted to pursue. He had always been friends with this girl. She was at the top of her class, too. And very beautiful. But she was small for a Prymiahn woman. So he felt like he would never be able to have her because of his size.'

'Was it Kiisma?'

'Yes. All of her friends were curious if he would approach her. But she had already decided that she loved him years before. She was still afraid that she would not be able to accommodate him. But she was as close to him as I was. So she visited his home one day.

'His mom and dad met her and asked her to sit down. He had already told them of his intentions. They understood what it would mean for her because his father was substantially sized as well, but his mother was suitable to him. They told her that he would love to see her, and that because they were older, they would allow them to handle matters in their own way.

'Elrek told me that when Kiisma came into his room he was embarrassed, which is unusual for our people, but in his case, I understood. His folds were still swollen with arousal, and he was unprepared to see her. He said she just went up to him and kissed him on the forehead, lowered his pants and began slowly licking his folds until they popped. He said it took her an hour. Then she simply started telling him about how things were going at school. She did this every day for two weeks. Elrek said he finally began to feel better. He said that she told him the last day before he returned to class for his last sessions that if he wanted to proclaim her as his, she would accept publicly and proudly.

'Traditionally, the proclamation of marriage is done in public, and usually happens a day or two after the revelation. As I have told you before, it may be decades before the marriage takes place, but we choose our mates when we are young. Elrek told me that he did not want to proclaim Kiisma to have her refuse him in public, which he expected her to do because of his size. So when she told him that night that she would accept him, he determined that he would never hurt her. So he began cultivating a psychic link between himself and his symbiote.'

'I didn't know that was possible.'

'Most don't know how. But Elrek went to see Varek and Varek had some old books about the process. Elrek became a scholar of pleasure. He was already in love with Kiisma. So he learned to lean into the feeling of arousal and not be in a hurry. Kiisma's parents allowed her to visit Elrek occasionally-thanks to Varek's assurances that it would be necessary for her to learn certain things about her fiancé as well. So Kiisma would go to Elrek and then they would go into his parents garden. Elrek would then manipulate Kiisma's folds until she was just about to have an orgasm, then he would stop.'

'So Kiisma was as miserable as Elrek?'

'Yes. But she learned to anticipate it. They were both very much in love with each other. But Elrek's symbiote stayed aroused within him for 10 years until their Vrek-mal. Kiisma experienced no pain. Her pleasure was too great. And when the time came, she was so aroused that her seal was already opening in anticipation. She was so hungry for him. Her friends were jealous. But none of them want to experience pleasure torture like she has become accustomed to. Elrek is quite skilled at it now.'

'That explains so much. I'm still quite unsettled. But weren't you afraid for me?'

'I was concerned. I was not afraid. I knew Elrek would know exactly what to do. He waited over two years for you, and he was not going to make you experience anything but the best of himself. No female that he has ever been with has experienced any pain. But the pleasure he gives is almost unbearable. The women that he has had have felt that once was more than enough. I have been told that the throbbing that takes place afterward lasts for days. But he has stoked a fire in you as well, hasn't he?'

'Yes. He taught me something about myself I did not expect. The thing is, I did not know about his size until it was over. It was strange. It was if he knew that if I saw his -seye, I would abandon him.'

'Yes. That's how he prefers it. He only went on a few colonization missions when he was younger. Now he just serves as a scout. He prefers to mate his wife-and now you.'

'Jyn, I never realized how much he suffered. That explains his reaction at your first mission.'

'Yes. He is very tender with women. Doesn't matter which world. He knows more than most the damage that can be done when a male is overzealous. He is the best of us. He is well respected. I am glad that he pleased you, although I knew he would.'

'He did please me, Jyn. But I am glad to be home with you, now.'

This made Jyn feel wonderful. He didn't doubt her love. But part of him was worried that Elrek would completely seduce her.

'Careful, Jyn. Elrek has taught me how to capture thoughts more easily.'

Jyn smiled his approval. He said:

'I'm going to take you to bed and see what else you've learned. But first, I'd like to go see Alex and Lindsey, to see how they are adjusting.'

Morgan looked completely surprised at this. Elrek said:

'Remember Morgan, you have had two years to adjust. Alex and Lindsey are just now learning our ways.' Morgan said:

'I couldn't agree more. Let's go.'

CHAPTER SIX

WHEN MORGAN AND JYN arrived at Alex's, it was unusually quiet. They hesitated because they thought the kids may be enjoying each other and didn't want to disturb them. Morgan said:

'Let's chime anyway. They may just be relaxing.'

When Alex opened the door, he was red in the face. He was clothed in sweatpants, but he was obviously quite erect. Morgan looked away and searched for Lindsey.

'Oh great, you old tomcat. What is it? My head is spinning.'

'Hello Alex. Why don't you come with me to the kitchen? I'd like something to drink. Morgan, please find our daughter.'

While Jyn went with Alex to the kitchen, Morgan found Lindsey in the bathroom, neck deep in the bathtub. She was crying.

Morgan came in and closed the door behind her.

'Mom.' She started sobbing.

'Oh, Lindsey. How badly did her hurt you?'

'It wasn't all his fault, mom. When we woke up, we were both insatiable. We couldn't stop. We kept going at it until I wasn't even wet anymore. And you know what? I am still horny as hell. I got in the tub to soothe myself. But it's not even helping.'

'Jyn wanted to come over. Now I know why. I brought something for you. It's the healing oils I used when Jyn first took me. And I have some healing lubricant. You will not stop wanting each other. It's the pheromones the Prymiahns release. Everyone on board is part of a couple and they mate every day. When I was on the compound it was awful. I had to take a healing bath every day just to prepare for sex that evening, and another after. And even though at first it was uncomfortable, after a while my body adjusted on its own and my desire increased. But Lindsey, it took a few days.'

'Mom. He felt bigger.'

'He is. Is he overly aggressive?'

Lindsey was silent.

'Lindsey. I know my son. He has always been high-strung. And he loves how strong you are. But he must learn to be less physical with you-especially now. Jyn will talk to him.'

'He won't like that.'

'He won't have a choice. Here's a towel. They stay warm here. Did you notice? Wrap it around yourself while I freshen your bath and put some oils in it. You will soak comfortably while we are here. Alex will leave you alone. Then after you start to feel better, rub some of this lubricant inside and out of your vagina. It will soothe you and it will arouse you so you can have sex again.'

'It seems impossible to be in this much pain and still want him.'

'I know. But you crave it, don't you?'

'A little. Yes.'

'You'll realize that those feelings are normal here. Relax into them, Lindsey. We didn't feel like this on Earth, and it's not just because our males are slightly larger here. Some of it is because as women, we were taught that intimacy is taboo. Especially if we allow ourselves to desire it. It will be uncomfortable at first, yes. But relax. Calm your mind. Each day will get a little bit better for both of you.'

'YOU GOT ME ON THIS God-forsaken ship, and now what is happening to my dick?!'

'Calm down, Alex. It's normal.'

'Normal? You call this normal? We are trying to kill each other by fucking ourselves to death! Lindsey is in the bathtub in tears and all I can think of is fucking her again. And my dick! What the fuck?! It's growing? Why is it growing? You mother fuckers are some crazy ass freaky sons of bitches!'

'Alex. Nothing can be done. The changes to your penis are permanent. It will not continue to grow, I assure you. But your DNA is enhanced here, and your entire body is changing. Lindsey will adjust. You feel unsettled because you've just arrived. Remember? I told you that you would feel strange the first couple of weeks. That is why we have kept little Mandy in stasis. Your mom is taking care of Lindsey right now. She will be ready for you when we leave. And you will put some of this on yourself. It will soothe you and make it easier for you to slip into Lindsey without hurting her as much.'

'Is this what you used on my mom you fuck?'

'No. We create our own lubricant. But this mimics it. Both of you will enjoy it. Now stop being an asshole. I can't take you seriously anyway with that huge dick floating in the air.'

They both started to laugh. But Alex didn't shrink one bit.

'This is embarrassing.'

'Not for me, Alex. It's normal. As I said, you'll adjust. Now I'm going to check on your mom and Lindsey. You are going to have a drink and sit perfectly still until we leave. By the time we go, you and Lindsey will feel like making love again. Your mom gave her some ointment and oils to use. The worst of it is over.'

JYN KNOCKED ON THE door. Lindsey was already neck deep in the bath and feeling much better.

'Morgan, I need to see my daughter. It is a personal matter.'

Morgan understood what Jyn needed to do and why.

'Lindsey. I need you to trust Jyn right now. He will help you.'

'Please stay, mom.'

'I'll be right outside the door.'

Morgan left and shut the door. But she sat on the floor so she could hear. Jyn knew she would and that was fine.

'I'm sorry that you are in pain daughter. How do you feel now?'

'Much better. The oils help. Why is this happening, Jyn?'

'It's our biology. It influences everything it touches, for better or worse. You and Alex will find that you enjoy each other more as time goes on, and he will learn to pace himself with you. But I need to help you just a bit. I need to give you some of my enzymes.'

'How will you do that?'

'I will retrieve some from my folds. Then I will place it inside of you with my finger. It will be fast, I promise.'

'Jyn. I'm afraid.'

'I know. I had to do this with one of my daughters after her Vrek-Mal. She was miserable with arousal, and even Prymiahns don't become proficient with lovemaking for quite some time. But this will not hurt. It is a tradition that fathers do for their daughters. It is an act of trust and protection.'

'How will that protect me?'

'If a man touches you without your desire, he will regret it and feel something he does not wish.'

'How?'

'It is an enzyme that produces a small, tender area. If you are being attacked or if a man tries to enter you without your consent, you will focus, and it will produce intense pain for him. But you will feel nothing. *He* will scream, though. But, when you are intimate with the man you wish to be close to, it will help you to stay moist for him. Close your eyes for me, daughter. And open up for me.'

'Jyn.'

'Lindsey. You will never endure this again. But you will thank me when you are with Alex. Please obey me.'

Lindsey closed her eyes and slowly opened her legs beneath the warm water. Jyn retrieved some of the fluid from his folds on the tip of his finger and quickly rubbed it inside of Lindsey's vagina. She felt a slight tingle and it was over.

'All done daughter. Now you'll dry off and use the ointment your mom gave you. We're going to change your bed linens and I will place you on your bed, so you are comfortable. Then we will leave. Alex has something to help too. Then you will call us to tell us how you are tomorrow. Okay?'

'Thank you Jyn. Okay. Jyn?'

'Yes.'

'Do you really love mom? Sometimes it feels like none of this is real. I wake up in a cold sweat, and before I can think of anything, Alex is on me like cat. My mind is so troubled.'

'Yes. I love Morgan, and I am *in* love with her. It's hard to describe to you because on Earth it's so different. We don't portion out our love. We freely give it. When I make love to Morgan, I connect with her mind and spirit, not just her body. So I feel every desire, moment of grief, her experiences, and her love for her family. For me, you are as much my daughter as the ones that carry my seed. And Alex is my son. I know he feels he hates me-and he does on the surface. But I also know that the love he has for Morgan is strong enough for you both to survive this experience. I love you both.'

Lindsey was amazed at how comfortable she felt with Jyn. He made her feel comforted, protected, and loved. Jyn left the bathroom and closed the door behind him. He saw Morgan standing with tears in her eyes.

'Why are you crying loved one? This is also who we are. As I have told Alex, we are not one big bedroom.'

'It's not that, so much Jyn. It is that I felt the love you have for her. Thank you.'

'Because you are my wife, she is my daughter, loved one. And Alex is my son. Let's make up the bed and leave, so our children may comfort each other. It will take some time, but they will adjust.'

As Morgan and Jyn walked back to their quarters, they were able to have a pleasant conversation. Jyn said:

'I think Lindsey is getting used to me. Maybe Alex will eventually.'

'I think so too. What exactly will that enzyme do?'

'It will create a small area inside of her. Since the enzymes belong to me as her father in law, they have a bit of my -seye in them. If she is attacked and focuses on that area. It will produce a stinging sensation on the penis or -seye. But when she is aroused, it will provide more moisture.'

'I didn't know you could do that.'

'It pleases me for you to see me as a father. Not just a rapist.'

'Jyn.'

'Well, every time I see Alex, he reminds me of the pain I've caused you.'

'Jyn. He is my son. He has always been protective of me.'

'It is as it should be, of course. But I just want him to know how much I love you.'

'I know how much. That should be good enough.'

'It is, I just can't imagine my life without you now.'

'Jyn. I know you love me. I am bound to you now. The only thing I would give you up for is earth. I must tell you that. That as much as I love you, I hate what your people did to my world. I would give you up to have my planet back the way it was. Can you understand that Jyn?'

'Of course I can. Why didn't you want to tell me that before?'

'Because I didn't want to risk losing you, and I didn't want to risk losing the power to make a change. At first, I wanted to use your lust against you, so I allowed myself to enjoy being with you. But really, I fell in love and had no choice. Can you see why I was conflicted and didn't want to tell you?'

'Yes. And you know that I understand why. And also that I agree with the actions you must take. It would be the best for our world that the colonizations stop. So you and I agree. Listen to me Morgan of Earth. I will love you forever. I can't explain it. I don't need to.'

'I have to tell you something else.'

'What?'

'I think Elrek is in love with me. Isn't that against the rules?'

'No. Not really. Elrek's position is as your consort, but how he feels about you is something he can't control. How do you feel about him?'

'I don't know.'

'Yes. You do. You don't want to love him, but you find yourself losing your will to him.'

'I don't like that feeling.'

'Why not? Does it change the way you feel about me?'

'No. That's what's strange. It's no different than the love I have for both you and Bruce. I love both of you but in different ways. You satisfy the pain aspect that I enjoy. Bruce satisfies the Terran in me. And Elrek has opened up another aspect I did not expect.'

'It is as it should be. But something else is in your mind I can almost catch.'

'I was thinking about how miserable he is most of the time. How he stays aroused. And after you told me his history, I feel I know why, and I think I have a solution. What would happen if we allowed Elrek to experience the Vrek-mal with me? I could be reconstructed like I was with you, and he could experience that part of himself finally.'

'That would require approval from the counsel. And me. You know how large he is. Vrek-mal would certainly damage you. Maybe beyond repair. He is our strongest Alpha. I don't know, Morgan. He would be considered your second -Shaed. He'll want to give you his fertile seed.'

'Jyn. I don't think he is capable of hurting me. Even if I am reconstructed. And his wife Kiisma would be considered your wife as well, would she not? I remember when we were back on Earth and had dinner together. There was a sexual chemistry between you two.'

'How do you know?'

'You don't need to be Prymiahn to see some things. Tell me.'

'Kiisma and I have always been curious about each other. Idra finds it humorous. She doesn't mind because being around Kiisma tends to arouse me and of course, Idra benefits from that.'

'Yes. So did I. I recall when we got home that night you were quite vigorous with me. I needed a longer healing bath the next day. Go on.'

'Kiisma is like you. She enjoys the pain aspect. But Elrek refuses her that because he is afraid he will hurt her. So one evening while we had just returned from a mission she asked me to ravish her.'

'Did you?'

'Yes. She went into their garden, and I gave chase. Of course, it wasn't a real chase. And I had wanted to be with her, and had just gotten back from a mission, so I was swollen with desire. When I got to her, I forced her. It was wonderful. She was intoxicating. And her ecstasy in finally feeling sexual pain was only stoked.'

'My god, Jyn! What did Elrek and Idra do?'

'Well, as it turns out, Idra was curious about Elrek. So they enjoyed each other while I was ravishing Kiisma'

Morgan just shook her head. Jyn laughed and continued.

'Idra said that Elrek drove her mad, but her orgasms were incredibly intense. She said it was enjoyable, but she preferred my techniques. Elrek said that Idra was too impatient. But Kiisma and I are awaiting another opportunity to enjoy each other.'

'So I have an idea. Kiisma and I could both be reconstructed. You can have another Vrek-mal, but with Kiisma. She will get to experience the holy pain that she couldn't with Elrek. Elrek can experience that with me. You and Kiisma will then be able to enjoy each other as much as you please. I would not interfere. Idra is quite taken with Bruce. I know because she has been sending messages to me almost daily about how much she loves his dick. It's really quite funny. It would seem this would be a solution for all of us.'

They had arrived at their quarters where Jyn finally released Jyn-seye completely.

'I see you are pleased with the thought.'

'Oh yes. I don't know what has me more aroused. The fact that you are Prymiahn enough to suggest it, the fact that Elrek has inflamed your passion, or the anticipation of a Vrek-mal with Kiisma.'

'The thought arouses me too. It pleases me because...'

And Morgan whispered a thought to Jyn about something she couldn't speak of.

This whispered thought given to Jyn caused Jyn-seye to swell even more with his fluid. Jyn took Morgan to the couch, bent her over and pulled her robe up. He was pleased when he placed his fingers inside of her and found her throbbing and wet. He also found it was just fine with her that he fucked her forcefully, allowing his thoughts to drift from her to Kiisma, and how lovely it would be to take her during Vrek-mal, and have her remain his. Morgan felt this thought and it pleased her because she would be able to be free in her feelings for Elrek and her thoughts of him caused her to throb even more. And both Morgan and Jyn-Shaed made a wonderful orgasmic mess.

CHAPTER SEVEN

OF COURSE THE COUNCIL approved. But they wanted the Vrek-mals to happen quickly so that the Revered Mother could be presented at the ceremony with both of her -Shaeds. It would be the talk of the whole planet. The Revered Mother would have two -Shaeds. Jyn would be Primary, and Elrek would be secondary, so his title would be Shaed-Elrek. Kiisma was nervous, but excited. Elrek though, was cautiously pleased. Right before the procedure, Elrek had a personal conversation with Morgan.

'Morgan, I am overwhelmed that you would give me such a gift. But I am afraid. I will not be able to control my -seye.'

'I know, Elrek. But you deserve to experience the Vrek-mal and so does your -seye. You are the highest Alpha. And my desire to feel your -seye take me is overwhelming. Remember, I enjoy the pain aspect.'

'I know, but even now, he is increasing in pressure.'

'He has honored *you*, Elrek, now you must honor *him*.'

ELREK AND MORGAN DECIDED that they would carry on the ceremony in the private quarters that had been set aside for them when she accepted him as her consort. She had been reconstructed the day before and had been ceremonially bathed. Dr. Ren stationed herself outside, just as she did when Morgan experienced her Vrek-mal with Jyn. Dr. Ren had attended to Jyn and Kiisma the day before and things went quite well. Apparently, Kiisma liked the pain aspect even more than Morgan. According to the Attendants assigned to them, they haven't eaten a meal in over a day. She was more concerned with what would happen on the other side of *this* door, though. She doubted that Morgan knew what she was in for.

MORGAN, LAY NAKED ON the bed. She was quiet. Elrek's face looked like a storm was behind his eyes. His folds were swollen so badly that she could not see any space between them and his -seye. His -seye hissed loudly and Morgan opened her legs. Elrek slowly crawled on top of her.

His eyes softened when they met hers. He saw complete acceptance there. And desire. He had never wanted or needed anyone as much as he needed her right now. He brushed her hair from her face. He saw her thoughts and released the symbiote.

Morgan allowed her mind to be free for Elrek to explore. She wanted him to know how much she trusted him. She allowed her body to relax and rest on the thoughts she had of him when they first met. The hidden desire she would not allow herself to fully feel. She wanted it to hurt just a little, enough for him to know that she was giving a part of herself to him that should have been his long ago.

The symbiote knew Morgan's thoughts as well and allowed himself to be free in his actions. It hurt and stung Morgan just enough to please, causing her to suck in her breath, but it wasn't quite as painful as she expected, probably because she was already so aroused in anticipation. When Elrek's -seye slowly pushed through her hymen, he would swell and force himself further in. He relished each movement he made, purposefully ravishing her slowly, just as she wished. Morgan felt the pressure and forcefulness with the pain, but the idea of him taking her in this manner continued to arouse her and even though it was uncomfortable, she found herself enjoying it. When he finally pushed through and began to thrust earnestly inside of her, Elrek's groans and grunts pleased her, and when he whispered her name in his own ecstasy, she had a warm and wet orgasm. There were no bad memories. No feelings to suppress. She loved Elrek. She felt fulfilled. Even Jyn-Shaed didn't ravish her like this. It was as though she had always loved Elrek, and he was always the one that should have been hers, even before Bruce. She didn't understand how it could be. Elrek was huge inside of her. She could still feel him throbbing.

'I can't get enough of you.' He whispered breathlessly in her ear.

She felt the same. No more lessons to learn. Just love to feel.

'Is this what Vrek-mal truly is?' She whispered to him.

'Yes.'

She knew it was the truth. This is what it should be between two people who love each other.

This is what she saw in the vision when Elrek was chasing Kiisma. The purity and simplicity of being with someone you love, bonding with them, starting a family with them. All of life in one moment of time.

'Morgan, are you now my wife?'

'Yes, Elrek. And are you now my husband?'

'As I have always been, I will be forever.'

'I am going to give you a gift, at first it will cause much pain, but after, you will experience ecstasy that no other woman on Earth or Prymiah can claim.'

'It is as it should be, Elrek-seye. I will receive your gift.'

Elrek-seye then released the spines on the head of his -seye and pierced the top half of Morgan's vagina. Then he caused the spines to throb and release his essence into her. Small tentacles emerged to cover the spines as he pressed them into her flesh. It felt like multiple needles piercing her insides.

'Elrek.'

'Yes. I am giving you a -seae. But not transforming you completely. You will feel pleasure from two worlds. Yours and mine. True balance.'

And in that moment, the spines retreated and Elrek began to thrust more gently. As he rubbed his substantial length along Morgan's vagina, his head manipulated her -seae. She began to convulse with the orgasm of her vagina, but afterward she felt a different feeling, a gentler orgasm, but continuous.

'Elrek is this the seae-bereth?'

'Yes. The orgasm of our females is more sustained, but the contractions of your own vagina are strong and intoxicating, They cause me to lose myself in your pleasure. Still your mind. What do you feel?'

'Your -seye is throbbing with the -seae you have given me. It's-it's wonderful.'

'What else?'

'We are in sync with the heartbeat of the ship!'

'Yes! This is how it is on our world. It is wonderful to be inside of you. To feel your welcoming heat. You are my home, Morgan of Earth.'

They drifted off to sleep with Elrek still inside of her, as she continued in her seae-bereth.

After an hour or so, Elrek awakened to find Morgan looking at him lovingly. He thought to himself that he had never seen a woman so beautiful.

Morgan nodded to his folds. They were completely flat and his -seye was completely hidden and satisfied.

'Morgan. My wife. Elrek-seye is no longer swollen within me. He is satisfied for the first time. I have never felt so light. So free.'

Tears began to stream from his eyes.

'How are *you*, my wife?'

'I am fine, my -Shaed. I'm not in pain, just pleasantly sore. I enjoyed the Vrek-mal. And the seae-bereth. Your size pleases me.'

Dr. Ren knew this would be a good time to enter.

'I see you both have completed the Vrek-mal. Morgan you look amazingly well. Let me look.'

Morgan opened her legs for Dr. Ren to examine her.

'There's absolutely no damage. No tearing and no redness. But I see you were given a gift. Did you expect this?'

'No. I did not. I had a suspicion that Elrek's symbiote would finally calm down, though.'

'A couple nights worth of healing baths should still suit you both. But I see no reason you can't continue to enjoy each other as you see fit. You might as well. Kiisma and Jyn-Shaed are wearing themselves raw, I think. It is as it should be.'

And it was. Morgan and Shaed-Elrek enjoyed each other thoroughly for the next week, as did Jyn-Shaed and Kiisma. They all knew that when they returned to each other there would be much pleasure to be experienced, and their wedding night would be legendary.

They were only a month away from Prymiah.

A WEEK LATER, JYN AND Morgan returned to their routines. Elrek and Kiisma where in their quarters as well, and both couples spent time reacquainting themselves with each other. Both couples were overcome with passion and spent much of their time in bed.

Jyn said:

'I never thought in my lifetime that I would feel such satisfaction. My love for you has only grown.'

'I know how you feel. Jyn. But I am concerned that Alex will be completely undone.'

ALEX WAS STILL ANGRY about being on the ship. He didn't like the way it felt. It was almost like he weighed nothing at all. There was a constant throbbing that he couldn't hear, but he could feel. And everything had a glow around it. It was disorienting. Lindsey and Mandy seemed to love every aspect of it, but he felt out of place and clumsy.

There were good things about it, though. It was nearly always quiet. Prymiahns were open minded, but did not like being a disturbance to others, so soundproofed family areas were par for the course. Mandy had other children to play with, too. She attended pre-school with one of the other girls and because she had already been used to being around Jyn, she didn't notice their differences at all. And she was already picking up some Prymiahn words.

Mandy was also watched carefully. Prymiahns let their children explore, but there were always adults around. He found it amazing at how protective they were of the children. They were not strict in the sense of the word, but the children seemed to know their boundaries, and all were well behaved and seemed quite happy.

Mandy knew where Jyn and Morgan's residence was and since there were only royal family members on their deck, she would visit them often. Alex was afraid that she would interrupt them at some inappropriate time, but she never did, and she always came back with a full stomach and ready for a nap. Morgan told him that Jyn loved to chase her and play kitty cat with her. Alex asked him didn't he think that was kind of racist, but Jyn just laughed and told said, 'Well. We *are* inherently feline, so the little one is just recognizing that in us. Besides, it's fun!' Alex just simply did not understand his stepfather.

As he was approaching the dojo, he calmed down a bit. He realized that this was a moment that most people would kill for. Being on the starship of an extraterrestrial race, and not only that, being part of a prominent family. Still, he would trade it all for a chance to get back home and smell fresh cut grass and throw a ribeye on the grill.

When he entered the dojo it was very still. He noticed that there was no throbbing feeling here, no auras. He felt more grounded. The gravity felt like earth.

'Go ahead. Walk around.'

Alex jumped out of his skin. It was Elrek.

'Dammit Elrek, you scared me. What's with you people sneaking around.' Elrek chuckled.

'That's just how we move. You'll learn the same skill. I set the atmosphere to resemble earth. You may use this area as a place when you need to think without having any Prymiahn interference. The only time I'll be here is when I'm training you. This is your personal space.'

'It's huge, Elrek. Why so much space for me?'

'Once you start training, it won't seem as much. There are showers and a resting area in the back with a bed. There's even a place you can take your meals if you like. Space travel can be difficult-even for us. We detest it generally. So we try to make it as close to home as possible. We have our own areas. This one was made for you. We asked your mom what you may like. How did we do?'

Alex felt a pang of anger for a moment, then sadness.

'It's fine Elrek.'

'I *thought* you'd be angry when you heard.'

'What? That you are *also* my mom's husband? Yeah. It made me sick. But I am out of people to be angry with. My parents are caught up with you people. My daughter is learning your ways and your language before she even knows her own. My wife wants to try all of your foods. She loves the idea of being on a spaceship.

'Then I heard that mom did -what's that-the *Vrek-mal* with you? More pain?'

'Yes. It honored us both.'

'How is pain honorable? Do you know how many years Dad had to love on mom before she got over the pain other dudes put her through? Now this!'

'It's not the same, Alex. You don't understand yet. But you will. Spend your anger on our workouts.'

'I just don't know anymore, Elrek. I don't know if I have the energy.'

'You must. You will fight enemies much stronger than you. I cannot allow you to leave our world without being prepared.'

'This is not my fight, Elrek.'
'It was always meant to be your fight, Alex.'

CHAPTER EIGHT

ELREK TRAINED ALEX harder than most. 10 hours a day was considered light training. Elrek changed the atmosphere in the dojo every 2 hours. He changed the gravity every thirty minutes, and he could even change the grip on the floor. Alex would come in dressed in the traditional training uniform of the Vok-Tor, but by the time it was over, he would be soaked in sweat and dressed in nothing but his boxers. Elrek would look like he just came out of a salon-not a hair out of place and not one bead of sweat. But Alex was determined to learn. He still could not get the movements quite right, though and he had experienced more cuts than he wished. Vok-Tor training used live blades.

Elrek knew Alex wasn't focused. He thought he knew why.

'Alex. Why are you so undisciplined today? You are barely listening to my instructions, and you aren't even pretending to try.'

'I just want to go home. I'm tired.'

'So is Lindsey. Why don't we take a meal here before you go home?'

'What do you know about how tired Lindsey is?'

'Your mother speaks to me. She says she has visited Lindsey, and the oils and ointments are not helping Lindsey heal from your intimate activities as much as we had hoped.'

'I love my mom, but she talks too much. It's none of your concern.'

'Anything that involves your fighting skill is my concern. You are undisciplined in fighting and in matters of love. You are going to damage your wife. You leave here every night and take her roughly. She allows it because she knows you need to let off steam. Why are you so angry?'

'You're kidding, right? Look at what you people have done! To my family! To my world! You ask me why I am angry? I want to kill everyone who has a part in this. And I... I...'

'You couldn't stop it. You feel you should have been able to help your family. And then the only thing you have that makes you feel connected is the relationship you have with Lindsey. Don't you believe that if you continue to hurt her physically, that eventually you will damage her heart?'

'I can't help it Elrek. This place-this ship-it makes my head my spin. I feel out of control all the time. When I get home I just want to feel something familiar. And I'm always aroused. I feel lost. I can't deny anything you are saying, though it hurts me to admit it to you of all people.'

'You will leave now and go home. Clean yourself but don't touch your wife. I mean it. If you touch her, I will cut you in a tender place. You and Lindsey will come to my residence in two hours. I will arrange for an Attendant to watch Mandy for the rest of the week. We will be arriving in Prymiah week after next and I want you to be ready for more extensive training.'

'Why do you want us to come over?'

'Training.'

LINDSEY WAS HAPPY TO get out. She spent her days visiting Morgan and Jyn and getting accustomed to the ship. But during the evenings she felt she needed to take care of Alex. He was always angry. And he was always rough. She went through several jars of the ointment her mother-in-law gave her, and even used the technique Jyn taught her to make herself more lubricated. But she never used her skill to sting Alex. She felt that her duty as his wife was to accommodate him. She had already bathed and used the last of the ointment and was hoping it would be enough. When Alex came home and said they would be going out he looked tired and resolved. But at least he didn't come through the door aroused. Maybe she could have a little Prymiahn wine and relax enough to get through one evening without pain at least.

WHEN THEY ARRIVED AT Elrek and Kiisma's residence, They were surprised to see the couple dressed in sheer garments that left absolutely nothing to the imagination. Elrek's hair was tied in a ponytail but unbraided and his wife had arranged her hair the same way. Lindsey was astonished at how beautiful Kiisma was but confused because she was in human form. They both stood at the threshold with their mouths open. Kiisma said:

'Please come in, and welcome. I see you are a bit confused. It is as it should be. Come.'

'Elrek, Alex said. 'What is going on? You said we needed to come for training.'

'And that is exactly why you both are here. Lindsey, I apologize for not giving you notice. But it would seem you are in a dire circumstance.'

Lindsey blushed and sniffled back a tear.

'You both must understand that we care about your family very much, and by extension-you. Your well-being is important to us. And because I am uniquely qualified for this task Alex, my wife and I have agreed that we will teach you the method to bring your wife to seae-bereth.'

'What the hell is that?'

Alex was dumfounded, but a knotted pit started to grow in his stomach. Kiisma spoke:

'We are going to show you how to pleasure you wife.'

'Like hell. I think I know how to do that just fine.'

Lindsey started to cry in earnest now. Alex looked at her in shock. It wasn't that he didn't understand that he was hurting her. He just felt like he didn't know what else to do. And now he was embarrassed.

'Alex, as a man, I understand more than most how difficult it is to contain your passion-especially when you need to let off steam. But you must learn how to focus these energies, not only for your own pleasure, but the pleasure of your wife and her continued ability to accommodate you. Please follow me.'

While the men left the room momentarily, Kiisma and Lindsey had a chance to speak to each other earnestly.

'Kiisma, I don't know about this.'

'You aren't comfortable. I understand. But this is normal for our people. We teach our children when they are about to be married about our bonding techniques. It is important to learn because the females can be damaged if the males are too eager. Since our males see being able to enter us as honorable and holy, it is an abomination for them to cause us pain unless we wish it. And you are in much pain. And even though you love Alex, you do not wish it.'

'Yes. I am so glad to be here. Just to not have to be with Alex tonight. I am so raw. I am almost swollen shut. I'm embarrassed to be telling you this.'

Kiisma chuckled.

'You have nothing to be ashamed of. We will begin shortly.'

'Where did the men go?'

'Elrek went to show Alex his -seye.'

'Why would he do that?'

'You see how much larger Elrek is than I?'

'Yes. I've noticed.'

'Elrek has a very large -seye. Elrek wanted Alex to understand in the most basic way possible that if he can enjoy me without damaging me then it is absolutely possible for him to do the same for you.'

'He's never hurt you?'

'Never. Not even during our Vrek-mal.'

'Why are you in human form tonight?'

'It's quite simple. Your husband needs to see how to pleasure a vagina.'

Lindsey blushed deeply and as she did, Elrek and Alex reentered the room. Alex was white as a sheet.

Elrek said:

'Alex please come to our bedroom now. We have arranged seating for you both, but Alex you may have to observe a little more closely. So be prepared for that. There is nothing to be ashamed of, but you will be expected to observe and learn. And Lindsey will be the proof that you have listened, and I will be able to tell as you train.'

Lindsey and Alex were led to seats right at the foot of the bed. Both looked absolutely petrified. Elrek lovingly removed Kiisma's robe, and she stood beautiful and naked before them. Elrek did not remove his pants, but he took off his shirt. He then directed his wife to lay on her back with her legs opened up in front of Lindsey and Alex. Her vagina was clean shaven. Lindsey was fascinated that she looked so human. Alex was still in shock. Elrek growled softly and lovingly at Kiisma, which sent a tremor through Lindsey.

Elrek said:

'Now Alex. When you come home and you take you wife to bed, when she opens up to you like this, what do you do?'

Alex was silent. He knew but he didn't want to say.

Elrek said:

'Lindsey, what does Alex do? Tell me child.'

Lindsey was fighting tears because she didn't want to embarrass her husband. This was an impossible situation, but as she was struggling, she still felt her own soreness and the dread she felt when seeing her husband. Then she looked at Elrek and saw anger in his eyes as he looked at Alex. Finally, Lindsey said:

'He shoves it in and thrusts until he's done. I try to make myself think about things that arouse me. Sometimes it works. It's been easier since we've been on the ship and the ointments help. But he's so large and so aroused, I don't think he can help it.'

'He can help it. He just doesn't understand how yet. Alex, it is only because of my love for your family that I don't cut you to bits. But we are here now. And it is as it should be. Now watch. Kiisma has opened up to me, so she has submitted, just like your wife. But that doesn't mean that she is ready. And your arousal doesn't mean you are ready either. Arousal just indicates that you are physically able. Not that you are ready. Kiisma is not ready. Let's help her.'

Elrek got down on his knees and leaned into Kiisma's vagina.

'See how I gently part her labia with my fingers. I want to see her. You must watch what happens to Lindsey's vagina as you pleasure her. But you will only use your fingers to part her labia. Do not use your fingers inside of her. First you will use your mouth and tongue. And I have seen Terrans with their tongue work. You move too fast and too quickly. You don't enjoy the process. Watch.'

Elrek then began slowly licking Kiisma's labia moistening them with his tongue. Then he tickled her clitoris by slowly licking upward and tickling it at the tip. He suckled on it until Kiisma started to groan a bit. Then he stopped again parted her lips gently to see how he was progressing. After he did this, he earnestly put his entire mouth on the surface of her vagina and began licking and sucking very slowly and very deliberately until Kiisma started wiggling in earnest. Then he stopped from his work and spoke again.

'You will continue to lick her until she begins to glisten a bit. But she is still not ready. Look. She is moist, but not wet. By now you will be quite hard, and miserable with arousal. But you are not ready either, even though you may believe you are. Now I will use my tongue inside of her. I will move it slowly in and out until I begin to taste her fluids. Do it slowly and then more quickly until she starts to have an orgasm. Then stop.'

Elrek began to work this very magic on Kiisma and began to groan in pleasure himself. When she started to call his name he stopped because he knew she was about to release. When he rose from her vagina, she was quite swollen with desire and very wet. Elrek licked his lips and hissed at his smiling wife. Then he said:

'She was about to orgasm. But she still wasn't ready for me. Now I can use my fingers without causing her any discomfort. She is wet and aroused enough for me to reach her tender areas. One finger at a time.'

Elrek began to finger is wife. At first one finger teasing her clit and moving in and out of her vagina, teasing her G-spot. Her wetness was audible in the room, her scent intoxicating. Then he placed another and so on until he was thrusting three fingers inside of her. Finally he released his fingers and began using his mouth again and Elrek and his wife became lost in her orgasm. Elrek then raised up and Kiisma sat up opening her legs to show Lindsey and Alex her dripping, satisfied vagina. He said:

'Tell them how you feel my love.'

'Fully prepared to receive you, Elrek.' Lindsey said:

'But if you've come already, do you still want to have sex?'

'Oh yes. That is just my first orgasm. On a normal night, I will have three or more.' Elrek said:

'Alex. A woman's orgasm is not the end of her desire but the beginning. Her body has received pleasure for the sake of you wanting to show her how much you are willing to serve her needs. When she sees that, when she believes it, then she will be ready to receive you inside of her, no matter your size. You will begin to look forward to making love with her-not because you will be able to experience the orgasm, but because you want to show her how much you can pleasure her. Did you have an orgasm watching us, Lindsey?'

Lindsey was embarrassed at this question. She had lost herself in watching them.

'Yes.'

'Good.' He then looked at Alex.

'Alex. I already see the effect on you. It is as it should be. Now I will give you some rules for the next three days.'

Alex was too dumfounded to respond. Amazed. But dumfounded. Elrek continued.

'Alex, you will pleasure your wife for the next three days. You will observe how she likes to be touched and you will follow her lead. But you may not under any circumstances enter her until the fourth night. I don't care if you get as hard as those oak trees of yours on earth. You will come to the dojo an hour earlier and leave an hour later. I will observe your behavior and that will determine how your training proceeds. But if I ever see your wife in tears again because you have fucked her raw, I will punish you with your training and of that you can be certain.'

Lindsey asked, 'Elrek, what do I do?'

'Daughter, you are to do nothing but what you have always done. Be a beautiful, deserving wife. You owe him nothing. Your submission to him honors him. Let *him* honor *you.*'

This cut Alex to the quick. But he couldn't help but agree. Although he knew the next few nights would be a nightmare. Elrek said:

'Good then. Give Kiisma and I a chance to freshen up. The Attendants are preparing a light meal for us. We will eat and enjoy each other's company. Kiisma has given me an appetite and I'm hungry.

ALEX DIDN'T FEEL MUCH like eating. It was all too much. It wasn't even what he just witnessed between Elrek and his wife. It was what he saw in the other room. Elrek showed him his -seye. He had only seen two. The one from the rapist that he shot on his property, and the one from the Prymiahn Jyn killed in his and Lindsey's bedroom on Earth. When they got to the other room Elrek said:

'I need to show you my -seye.'

'Hell no, Elrek. I don't need to see that damn thing.'

'Yes. You do. There is a reason for everything I do.'

Elrek released his pants and revealed his folds. Nothing special there. They looked like the folds of all Prymiahns. Then something crawled out. Elrek-seye's head was the first thing Alex saw- it was as thick as a summer sausage but iridescent. The head covered a full third of the length of the -seye and was covered in spines. The length of it seemed to never end. He was afraid it was going to drape to his knees. But what would live in Alex's nightmares for a while was the mouth. The damned thing actually had a mouth. And inside of it were teeth. Sharp ones with canines as big as what should be on a full grown man.

And if that wasn't enough-could there be more? It hissed loudly at him. Alex jumped out of his skin.

'Elrek. What the hell!! What the hell, Elrek! Is that your dick?!' My mom?! I'm gonna kill you motherfucker, right now!'

Elrek caught Alex by the neck.

'You will calm down. Your wife is in the other room. I will not have our wives upset.'

Alex knew when Elrek was serious. He stopped yelling, but he did not calm down. Elrek understood this was a shock. His -seye retreated to its folds.

'Your mother felt no pain from my -seye, Alex. Only pleasure. I had to show you. You see how lethal he is. You see his size. My wives have never felt pain. And yet, I have been completely inside of them both. I show you because you also, are quite large and I know your passion runs deep. I wanted you to see that if I can control the desire of my wives so that they receive nothing but pleasure-even at my size-then you can as well. I see you understand.'

'I understand now. Dammit Elrek. Dammit. You people are fucking lethal. Your wife is so small. Okay. I get it. But how does this tie into my training?'

'You'll see.'

CHAPTER NINE

WHEN ALEX AND LINDSEY got home it was very quiet. Mandy was staying in the quarters of her new friend and since they had met her parents already and they were on the same deck, they felt she would be safe, comfortable, and well fed. But it was almost too quiet.

'Alex, I'm sorry.'

'No Lindsey. I'm sorry. For all the years I've hurt you.'

'You never laid a hand on me. You've always been a good provider. And you're a wonderful father.'

'You know what I mean. All those things are valuable, but I'm a selfish lover.'

Lindsey was quiet. Alex left the room for a moment. When he returned he had on some crazy looking shorts that were obviously too small.

'What's with the shorts?'

'Well, while I was in the other room getting scared to death by Elrek, he told me that you are not to see me aroused tonight or tomorrow night. He said you've seen enough of my erections for a while and to give you a break. You're smiling and blushing a bit, so I take it you agree.'

'I'm sorry. But yeah. I'm a little raw.'

'He wants me to go down on you tonight. He said you might not be able to have an orgasm, but he said he believes it will help and he gave me a different ointment to use starting tomorrow. Are you up for it?'

'Yes. Raw or not, after seeing what we just saw, I'm a little turned on.'

'It was like looking at a live porno wasn't it? I couldn't even speak.'

They both laughed, but they were nervous. Alex was already painfully erect. And Lindsey was afraid he would lose patience.

But Alex took his time. He found himself enjoying hearing Lindsey moan and seeing her get more and more wet. His dick hurt, but he remembered that it was part of the process of giving her pleasure. And Lindsey did have an orgasm. This pleased Alex. He crawled into bed next to her and they both fell asleep. By the time the alarm went off the next morning, Lindsey was already in the kitchen fixing breakfast.

'Good morning, Lindsey. Why up so early?'

'Hi sweetheart. I know you have to get to the dojo. I thought you might like something to eat. They actually gave us bacon! I found it in the back of the walk in.'

'Wow. It's been a minute since I've had bacon. Maybe a couple slices and your eggs that I love. Then I'll hit the shower and you can have the day to yourself. How do you feel, Lindsey?'

'Wonderful Alex. Just wonderful.'

As Alex was walking to the dojo, he felt conflicted. He still did not understand the meaning behind all of this. But Lindsey seemed like a different woman. She was glowing. She didn't walk like she was in pain. But as Alex got closer to the dojo, remembering how he pleasured his wife and her reactions began to arouse him again, and his dick was straining at the shorts. He finally arrived. Elrek had been there already. He just stood there and looked at Alex as if he was examining him. Alex figured that's just what he was doing.

'Good morning, Elrek.'

'Alex. How was your evening?'

'It went well.'

'I see. I have something for you before we begin our training.'

'Oh?'

'Yes. Those shorts you are wearing to control your arousal won't do. They are too restrictive. There is no need for you to experience pain. I left some shorts made from the same material that I used to bind my folds before my revelation. The fabric is extremely strong, but lightweight. It has some give. You will be able to wear them to bed and be comfortable no matter how aroused you become. Also they will protect you while you and I spar.'

Alex went to the rear to change and when he put on the shorts he felt such a relief. They did not bind him too tightly but secured him enough to provide the protection he needed. They were cool to his skin, and he felt himself take a deep breath once they were on.

'Thanks, Elrek. That *is* much better.'

'Good. Let us begin the next phase. Today your mind is chaos. You know your task. But you are unsure if you can complete it. That is how you felt with Lindsey last night, was it not?'

He continued without letting Alex answer.

'Imagine in this moment, it is your first battle. You are unfamiliar with the battlefield. The surroundings don't feel like home. You don't know your boundaries. You haven't seen your opponent yet, but you know he is there. Right now, I want you to familiarize yourself with your surroundings. Just take slow deliberate breaths.'

Alex had already had extensive martial arts training on Earth. And he had always been high strung. His sensei gave him breathing exercises to do before and after training to center his thoughts. He realized this was very similar. He did feel chaotic. Since last night he felt like he was going down deeper into a rabbit hole-so deep that he could never find his way back. Elrek sensed his thoughts.

'That's right, Alex. Just like when you were on Earth. It doesn't matter what is going on around you. You know your own heart, your own abilities. It doesn't matter where you are. You control your breathing; you control your emotions. You control your reaction to any environment you are in. Even now. Look around you. This is your enemy's domain. But it doesn't matter. Your enemy does not know you. Seek the enemy in his own domain. Overtake him.'

'How Elrek. How do I do that when my enemy is so much stronger.'

'All adversaries have a weakness. But you are not here to focus on the strength of your enemy. You are here to focus on your own strengths. You will learn how to focus chaos.' Elrek continued:

'When you see the battlefield for the first time, you are at your most alert. Your eyes want to dart everywhere. You are looking for the enemy. You are unfamiliar so you are poised to pounce. You must learn to change that way of thinking. Slow your breathing. Take your time. See everything around you. Where are your footholds? How does the air feel? What do you smell? What do you hear? Slowly take it all in. Learn how to move quietly. Effortlessly. Close your eyes. Don't open them. Let your arms fall to your sides. I will move around you. When you start to feel where I am, block me with your outstretched arm, palm outward. That's all we will do today. You will stand there. Eyes closed. Breathing soft. We will cease when you have touched me.'

Elrek had already started darting around Alex as he was speaking. Sometimes close enough for his breath to move Alex's hair. Sometimes just behind him. It was two hours before Alex knew Elrek was already moving. But he kept his breathing slow and centered.

A while after that, Alex found his mark. He struck Elrek on the chest. Five seconds after that, Alex fainted.

'Elrek. What happened?'

'You reached the point where your mental awareness surpassed the physical. Once you got there, you found me.'

'Why did I pass out?'

'You didn't really pass out. Your mind had no need for your body. So, it put it to rest. You will learn to remain standing when this happens. You are simply not used to it yet.'

'I needed this Prymiahn stuff at home when we had our exhibitions!'

'Alex. This was always inside of you. I am just bringing it out. Tomorrow I will use my short blade. For greater incentive.'

'You are finally going to kill me.'

'Not at all.' Elrek chuckled. 'You will be ready.'

As Alex was walking back to his quarters, he was amazed to realize that the feelings he had last night and the way he was taught to fight today really did tie in together. Everything mimicked how he felt about his relationship with Lindsey.

He had always loved her but seen her as mysterious and unknown. He never quite knew how to approach her. He didn't want to appear weak, even though he knew he could and would kill anyone that laid a hand on her. But out of his frustration, he was in a hurry to show her what he thought was the way she wanted to be shown. He never took the time to learn about her.

When Alex got home, Lindsey had a hot meal waiting for him. It was a lovely and quiet dinner. He found that he was not as anxious as before, but he did feel aroused as usual. Lindsey could always tell with him and was beginning to get a little apprehensive even though she was feeling much better. But this time Alex seemed calmer. When the time came, he led her to the bedroom and was pleased to see she did not have any panties on underneath her dress. He took off all of his clothes but left the undergarment on that Elrek gave him.

He was slow this time. Deliberate. He took his time enjoying how she felt, how she smelled. He tasted her for the first time since they've been married. He used his fingers to tell when she was tense or relaxed, and he would slow down when her breathing quickened. He listened to her moans and pleas for him to satisfy her, but even though his own arousal strained against the garment, he allowed himself to anticipate being with her. He kept pleasing her with his mouth and fingers until she came.

He ran her a warm bath and dried her off when she was done, then he showed her to bed so she could get some much needed sleep. Afterward he took a nice warm shower allowing thoughts of his wife to envelope his mind. He looked down at his throbbing dick and chuckled to himself.

'Throb on, little brother.'

ELREK STOOD JUST LIKE he did yesterday and looked at Alex. He said:

'It is as it should be.'

'Why do Prymiahns say that all the time?'

'Because we understand that there is nothing in life that happens by mistake. Even when we ourselves perceive mistakes in what we or others have made. When we go through difficult times, it gives us peace to know that even then, our lives are meeting a purpose greater than what we could possibly know.'

'Why did you look at *me* and say it just now.'

'Because I see your growth. I see your heart rate has slowed a great deal since yesterday. You are not in chaos. Your eyes show calm even though there are still emotions just below the surface. And you are not aroused. You have walked the length of this deck through our atmosphere and the pheromones that we give off early in the morning. Yet, you are centered and ready to train.'

'That's why you wanted me to come early and stay later.'

'Yes. The times I have you train are when we have our mating cycles. I knew you would be bombarded when you came in the morning and at your departure.'

'So it was a test.'

'Yes. Because of our biology, Prymiahns must learn to focus all of our energy in order to function and have an orderly society. Because we mate every day, we cannot avoid the emotions and drives that are part of that. So we must learn to manage them. That will be why it will be difficult to fight Prymiahns who have given themselves over to colonization. They have not only decided to give themselves over to their passions, but to the chaos that it brings.'

'You're telling me that if it were not for the Vok-Tor, you would be out of control as a people?'

'Yes. We all are practitioners of the Vok-Tor. It not only trains our bodies to fight, but our minds as well.'

'I'm beginning to see why you called the training you gave me with Lindsey the other night important.'

'Oh? Tell me.'

'Each time I am with her, I feel the training that I have had with you the previous day. Each time I feel closer to her, more understanding of her needs. I am beginning to feel that it is my duty to fulfill those needs, not just for my own gain, but for hers first and foremost. Then when I come here, I feel more centered because the journey to the fulfilled purpose is how I learn how to accept the result when I get there.'

'Good Alex. You are beginning to understand.'

'I still don't like you.'

'It is as it should be. Let's begin.'

This time Elrek trained Alex to avoid a strike. It was only the beginning of his training. First Elrek showed Alex defense moves and how important it was to learn to move slowly and then progress to the speed Alex admired so much. Elrek told Alex that knowing how the body would move if slowed would assist him with his speed. Alex didn't quite get it, but he knew it had a lot to do with pacing himself. And Elrek taught him it also had to do with disarming his enemy. If his enemy expected speed, he would fight against it. But if an imperceptible combination between speed and pace is used it will almost always keep the enemy from achieving the first strike. By the time it was over, Alex had several cuts, but not nearly as many as Elrek expected.

'They will quickly heal Alex-not even leaving a scar.'

'I don't think I get it.'

'You do. You just don't see it. But you will. Tonight, when you are with your wife, don't wear any clothing. Do not hide your arousal. Please her in every way except do not enter her with your penis under any circumstances. Let her see how aroused you are. What she has done to you. Show her by pleasuring her, but tonight, don't let her orgasm. Don't let her anticipate what you will do to her next.'

'That's cruel Elrek.'

'On the contrary. It is teaching her something as well. Lay next to her. Let her feel you against her. Let her touch you. She will try to entice you. If she tries to tempt you, arouse her again but leave her to burn in her desire. Come in extra early tomorrow.'

Alex did exactly what he was told. He was almost surprised that Lindsey pleaded and moaned for him to finish her. But what surprised him more was his erection. It was massive and thick. It felt like a steel pipe between his legs. His balls were so full. But he wasn't miserable. He was beginning to enjoy the challenge of it. He was enjoying seeing how long he could go. Lindsey was wide open and wet. She was up all night and when she tried to grind against him, he pushed her off and teased her with his mouth and fingers. And just when she was about to cum he left her to burn. Finally she drifted off to sleep.

CHAPTER TEN

WHEN ALEX ARRIVED AT the dojo, Elrek was waiting in his usual stance.

'How did Lindsey fare last night?'

'She's pleasantly miserable, I think.'

'Good. I see you are focused and confident. You are beginning to understand your connection with the Vok-Tor. Today, you will learn how to strike. I have your training weapon. Once you become familiar with it, you will attempt to strike me. Once you strike me, your training is done for the day, and you may leave and finally enjoy your wife completely. But let me ask you this. Do you believe you will hurt her again?'

'Never.'

'Why?'

'Because, I have gotten so much pleasure by learning how she responds to my touch. I love hearing her moan and feeling her breathing change. I love the different ways she smells depending on how aroused she is. I love her texture and how she contracts her muscles. I feel that I have so much more to learn about her. She is opening up to me. Trusting me.'

'And because she trusts you...?'

'I can trust myself.'

'Exactly. Now let's begin.'

Elrek changed the floor texture of the floor so that Alex's footing would not be certain.

'Elrek what is this now? How am I supposed to move?'

'Just like you did before, Alex. But faster. Remember how fast Jyn was at your home? This is part of it. You think the floor is in control of your movement, but you are always in control. You can use your circumstances to your advantage. If the floor is slippery use it to move faster. Remember how you had to stand still on your first day until you hit me? Use that same technique. Keep your eyes open while you try to stand in the circle without slipping and block me.'

Alex fell several times until he realized he was focused on the floor and not blocking Elrek. He remembered the first time he was in the dojo, and he could not block Elrek until hours had passed. When he forgot about his circumstances and worked on his instinct, he did much better. This time he learned faster. It was only two hours before he was able to block Elrek's hits. Then training was done for the day.

'Alex, you are improving each day. Your success will always depend on where your focus is. Your enemy will assume you are weaker. Let him. He will always believe he is stronger, and that is when you strike. Use their arrogance against them.'

'I think I'm beginning to understand Elrek.'

'You certainly are. I have been leading you around the dojo for the past few minutes. You haven't been thinking about the floor because you have been truly listening to me. The floor is slick as ice, but it didn't matter because you gave it no thought.'

'Wow. What's next? You've got me excited now!'

'Well, training is over for the day. I'm giving you a couple of days off. Your wife is waiting for you, and tonight you will finally get what you have been waiting for.'

Alex had forgotten all about Lindsey. It felt good to be free of sexual thoughts. But as soon as Elrek reminded him, all of his desire flooded back. He started to leave. Elrek said:

'Take a shower first. You won't have time to when you get home, and you smell.'

'I hate you.'

'I know.'

WHEN ALEX STEPPED THROUGH the door, it was quiet. And dark, except for the soft light coming through the bedroom door. As he got closer, he could smell Lindsey's scent. It was intoxicating. She was laying on the bed naked and glistening with sweat. He knew what she had been doing. But he wanted to tease her a bit.

'What have you done, baby girl?'

'I was waiting on you, Alex.'

'Open your legs and let me see.'

She did what she was told. She was throbbing with anticipation.

Lindsey spread her legs open, and Alex stuck a finger in.

'Oh that was easy, but I don't think you're quite ready yet.'

Alex put his mouth and tongue to work. Her pussy tasted so good. He slipped two fingers in. He knew exactly what to do. She was getting very wet. He stood up and took off his clothes. His hard dick hung impossibly in the air, seeming to defy gravity.

'Fuck me Alex.'

'Not yet. We're not nearly ready.'

Alex climbed on top of Lindsey and kissed her hard on the lips. Then he moved to her hard nipples and took them in his mouth in turn, sucking them hard and nipping them as he moved his mouth from them. Lindsey arched her back.

He then stuck his fingers inside of her again. Three this time.

'Alex, I'm gonna die!'

'No, no you won't.'

He took the head of his dick and rubbed it against her pussy without going in. Then he sticked it just inside and thrusted it back and forth going no deeper than the head. Lindsey tried to force it all the way in, but he pulled it back out.

'Stop, Lindsey. Don't rush.'

'Then let me suck it. You know you like the way I do it.'

He did indeed like the way she sucked his dick. She scooted to the end of the bed and grasped it firmly. She tickled the ridge of its head with her tongue before sucking it all the way in. Lindsey had no gag reflex. So she would take the whole thing in her mouth sucking, licking, and stroking it. Tonight she was especially hungry, and he came quickly. She swallowed every drop and sucked on it as she pulled it out. She had worked his dick so well, it felt like she was still sucking on it.

It didn't dampen his desire though, it stoked it. Under the bed was a nice sized dildo that would work just fine to give Lindsey her first orgasm and give him time to get hard again. It wouldn't take long. He returned to her pussy with gusto, sucking her clit and fingering her until she was sopping wet. Then he used a bit of the lubricant that Jyn gave them on the dildo and slowly pushed it in her pussy, moving it in and out until he thought she was close. Then he stopped.

'Get on your knees baby girl. Let me see if you are ready.'

Lindsey got on her knees and Alex spread her cheeks apart. She was coming along nicely. Lips swollen and pink and wetness leaking nicely from her pussy. He saw that her asshole was throbbing too. They never tried anal, but he found himself wanting to get to her ass. He finally stuck his extremely hard and throbbing dick slowly in her pussy and was pleased to hear her groan. As he thrusted inside of her, he slowly stuck a finger inside of her asshole and she groaned again. Alex thought that meant she wasn't ready, but when he removed his finger, she said:

'No Alex don't stop. I want to feel everything.'

Alex kept fucking her pussy until he was about ready to cum and then he pulled out. He put some lube on her asshole and some on his fingers. He told Lindsey to lay back down and open wide. He bent to her pussy again and began licking it and flicking her clit, and while he was doing that he stuck a finger slowly into her asshole. Then two. He started to thrust them, and Lindsey started to wiggle.

'Are you ready, baby girl?'

'I think so. Just go really slow.'

Alex started by slowly putting his head in and thrusting it in and out. Her ass started to loosen up a bit. Then he slowly pushed it halfway in. Her ass felt so tight and warm. He wanted to keep going, but he knew he had to take it slow. He pushed it slowly the rest of the way in, but he didn't thrust.

'I'm all the way in, baby girl. How is it?'

'It's tight Alex, but I'm so hot, I don't care.'

'Play with your pussy, Lindsey. Play with it until you almost cum, let's see if that helps. I'll leave it in until you tell me I can thrust. It feel so good being in your asshole, you're so tight and warm.'

Lindsey began masturbating vigorously and could feel herself get closer and closer. She started to focus on the fact that Alex was in her ass and that turned her on so much she got extremely wet.

'Fuck my ass, baby!'

Alex began to earnestly thrust, first slowly and then faster. He was surprised that she opened up even more and that thrusting was getting easier. He couldn't believe how good her ass felt. But before he came, he pulled out and finished up in her pussy. When he finally pulled out, they were both sweating and collapsed on the bed laughing.

'Well, Lindsey. Did I pass?'

'Oh yes, Alex. You passed. But there's always room for extra credit!'

CHAPTER ELEVEN

ONE MORNING, MORGAN woke up to find Jyn looking at her curiously.

'I know that look, my Shaed. What now?'

Jyn smiled.

'I have something to tell you.'

'Well?'

'Your male Attendant wants to bond with you. He views it as a gift, to pay homage to you as the Revered Mother.'

'Jyn, this goes too far. I feel like a walking pussy. No arms, no face, just a great big vagina.'

Jyn chuckled and growled the way she liked.

'Not at all. You should know at this point that bonding is a sacrament on our planet, and you are now the representative of our faith. And the Attendant is a High Priest. I know you enjoy his treatment of you. Especially how thoroughly he fingers you at the end of your bath.' Morgan blushed but then relented. She had some idea he knew, but they never spoke of it.

'I do.'

Morgan remembered the first time it happened. She had almost fallen asleep in the bath and was very relaxed. Her breathing was slow and steady, but she could feel heat building between her legs. Jyn had left to go to a meeting, and she was thinking that it would be a while before he returned to take care of her need. Just when she was about to open her eyes, she felt the Attendant's finger toy with her clit rings. She decided not to open her eyes. But she allowed herself to relax. He then slowly began rubbing his fingers along her hardening clitoris until she started to raise her hips upward, and before she knew it, he was three fingers deep and she lost control and began to thrust and groan against her deepening orgasm. When she finally opened her eyes, she found him looking at her deeply and lovingly, and just as abruptly as it began, it ended by him nodding to her respectfully and helping her out of the bath to dry off. Each time he serves her bath, he serves her pussy, whether Jyn is present or not.

'He'll be in this morning once I leave. He will not be what you expect. I'll return later this evening. Elrek wants to show me additional defense techniques anyway, so it works out.'

Morgan always takes a short nap when Jyn leaves for the dojo in the mornings. She enjoys the time to herself. She always expects the Attendant to come in and prepare her bath, so when she heard his footfalls as he came in, she did not stir. She had already forgotten the conversation she had with Jyn. She was simply too sleepy to care.

Just as she snuggled under the covers to continue her nap, she was met with a wonderful scent. The male Attendant was standing next to her bed. He had on a sheer green robe with gold filigree weaved throughout. His hair was loosened from its typical braid. He gently pulled the covers from Morgan's nude body. She raised up on her elbows, immediately remembering the conversation she had with Jyn earlier. He was beautiful. And unlike most mornings when he worked in silence, he was whispering just under his breath and in his own language. Each word sounded like a musical note full of harmonics, and Morgan found herself responding. She slid over and indicated that he should join her in bed.

The Attendant allowed his robe to fall and slid gently beside her. He put his lips to her ear and began whispering his song to her. She was about to know true bliss.

When Jyn returned later that evening, he found his wife in the dress that Elrek gave her before their first bonding, and the traditional robe that Jyn gave her on the day of their Vrek-mal. She was glowing like he had never seen her, and instead of desire, he felt reverence. He found a chair and fell into it. Then she came to him and sat at his feet.

'Morgan, you should not be at my feet.'

'I want to sit right here with you, my Shaed, and simply enjoy your company.'

'Tell me. What happened? This is also my first time experiencing something like this. You look amazing. And your scent is...making me feel drunk.'

'Jyn. I never knew what was possible in the communion between two people. He slid next to me this morning and his body heat was so powerful, I began to sweat. Then he began to sing into my ear, in Prymiahn. But it was barely audible. All I know is that the more he spoke the more I forgot where I was. I lost all sense of time. All I could focus on was the sound of his voice and the heat from his body next to mine.'

'So it is true, then.'

'What, Jyn?'

'Prymiahn Attendants pray in this way.'

'Who are they praying to?'

'Jali-Seae. The first Revered Mother. He was praying for her to show him the way.'

'The way to what?'

'Your pleasure.'

'That explains so much. He never stopped the entire time he was with me.'

'I'm sorry to interrupt. Please continue.'

'He started between my legs. I expected his touch to be the same as it is when he bathes me. Remember, he was still giving off body heat.'

'Yes. Go on.'

'His fingers were cool. But not painfully cool. The contrast between the heat his body was giving off and the temperature of his fingers was very stimulating. He stroked me firmly until I started to moisten. Then he released his fingers and lowered himself to use his mouth. Even his tongue was cool, and it seemed exceeding long, entering me almost like your -seye, or Bruce's penis, but so much more flexible and...'

'Hungry. Like he was never going to taste you again and...'

'He was savoring each moment. Yes. Then he raised himself on top of me and began singing in my ear again. While he was singing, he was fingering my right nipple. No sooner than I began to desire him to suck it, he did just that.'

'Morgan, he felt what you needed from him.'

'Yes. I was throbbing with desire, wet with it, but I had not had my first orgasm. He controlled that. Then once again he stopped and began his prayers again, and he became impossibly hot. Then I felt his -seye push slowly inside of me. That's not quite right. It pulsated and throbbed inside of me. Once it was all the way in, he lay perfectly still except for his singing. While this was happening, I felt his -seye moving inside of me. Finding every part of me and taking its time stimulating it. When I thought I would die from the pleasure, he released me to have an orgasm. But it was...'

'The Seae-Bareth.'

'Yes. My orgasm continued to flow from me as he pulled out.'

'But you did something he didn't expect, didn't you?'

'Yes. I was still experiencing the Seae-Bareth, and I felt so aroused in his presence. I still don't understand it completely, but I felt compelled to roll over and position my body in the submissive posture of the Vrek-mal.'

'Then what happened, Morgan?'

'His prayer song became louder and more melodic. It reminded me of when I used to feel ecstatic in my faith. When I would sing it would be louder and more passionate because I really felt connected. At that thought I became overwhelmed because I completely understood the emotion behind his song. But when he entered me this time it felt like he was entering me both ways. And instead of him being still, he began to thrust, but very slowly. At each thrust, the Seae-Bareth would be more intense. I felt it running out of me and down my legs. My vagina and anus were throbbing with pleasure. And then he released himself inside of me, but instead of it running out of me...'

'Your body absorbed it.'

'Yes. And when he came, he hissed. But it wasn't loud. It reverberated inside of me and made me tremble. Then we were finally done and both of us collapsed on the bed.

'The heat he was giving off began to dissipate, but before it did, he put his mouth to mine and kissed me deeply. Then he went to my ear and sung one more prayer. I feel into a deep sleep and when I awakened, he was gone. A bath had been drawn for me and these clothes laid out. After I had bathed and dressed, I noticed that a glass of Guardian fruit juice was waiting for me on the table next to the bed and I drunk it all in one gulp. I didn't realize how thirsty I was, but then I remembered what the Guardian fruit's purpose was. And I immediately felt better. Then you walked in. I still don't understand completely what happened to me.'

'Morgan. I don't believe either of us know the consequences of what just happened.'

'What do you mean?'

'Attendants do not speak-not because of subservience, but because they are the high religious sect of our High Temple. They are Temple Guardians and are one step down from the Supreme High Priest. Unless required of them, the only words they speak are words sung in prayer. They are very powerful.

When they are chosen, they spend years in the temple, not only learning our sacred practices, but learning the healing and sexual arts that are in the sacred books. They are the only ones allowed to read them. They are humble because they recognize how formidable they are. They never colonize, but they keep us cleansed spiritually. That is why we allow them to bathe us and serve us. They are not really servants, but...'

'Guardians.'

'Exactly. They make sure our motives are pure. It is also why you are allowed to read those books, although you haven't been given access to the more...explicit ones.'

'Why did I feel like he penetrated me-everywhere?'

'Your Attendant is unique. It is not for me to say. I would think at some point he will tell you. If it suits him'

'I am still throbbing, even though I've tasted the Guardian fruit. And Jyn-it's difficult for me to sit completely on my bottom. I mean, it was difficult when I was with you the first few times, but with the Attendant, it feels like he turned me inside out.'

'It is a mystery. Jyn-seye is swollen tightly within me. But he does not dare expose himself. I have a feeling this experience is not over for either of us. No one is even allowed to know the holy names of the Attendants but their spouses and the High Priest.'

Just then the door chimed. Jyn and Morgan got up to receive the guests, but they both had a feeling of who it was, and they still had pits in their stomachs.

When they opened the door, they were astonished at what was before them. The male Attendant and his wife stood in their priesthood regalia. Deep green robes of royalty with gold lettering delicately woven into the fabric. They were prayer verses. Underneath they wore similar garments to the ones that Jyn-Shaed wears when he goes on military missions. Both wore their long hair in high ponytails which they had draped across their chests. They had weapons. Lethal blades strapped on their hips. Neither Jyn nor Morgan had ever seen them like this. They each had beautiful green pendants on a delicate golden chain around their necks. They were holy royalty. The Attendant's wife held a long golden box which she handed to Jyn when they entered and shut the door. They did not speak. They dropped to one knee before Morgan and her -Shaed, then they rose and opened the box that Jyn was holding. It was an identical pendant to the one they each wore. The female gently and reverently took the pendant from its box and stepped to Morgan, who instinctively bowed her head to receive it. Once she clasped it on Morgan's neck, the female kissed her cheek, whispered a prayer in her ear and bowed. Then the male Attendant, still flushed from his time with Morgan, stepped to Jyn and whispered a longer prayer in Jyn's ear which made him flush and stumble backward. Then they both smiled gently at them and left.

'What just happened, Jyn?'

'I cannot say.'

MORGAN HAD JUST SPOKEN with Lindsey the day before and apparently Alex had done his job. They were getting ready to make the final jump to Prymiah, and that meant the wedding was closer than ever. She was getting nervous. Her stomach was in knots and the only time she relaxed was when her Attendant bathed her. Jyn said:

'You need to calm yourself. If it wasn't for your Attendant, you would be a nervous wreck.'

'And that's just it, Jyn. I don't know why it takes the Attendant to calm me.'

'He is your spiritual guide. He's doing his job. You are about to land on a new planet, attend a marriage ceremony bonding you to two men besides your husband, and your Attendant will calm you by making love with you.'

'What's happening to me?'

'You are becoming the true Revered Mother. On our world we know that women are complex. We know that it is impossible for one man to provide all of her needs. You represent the complexity of women. The power. The vulnerability. The sensuality. It pleases me and Elrek that you share yourself with us. It pleases us that your Attendant has blessed you with his seed. You won't feel so out of place when we arrive. Your adjustment will be easier than you think.'

Morgan felt so uncomfortable. She had been constantly aroused for the past few days. The Attendant would push her to sleep, and that seemed like the only time she could get any true rest. But the new folds that had grown were so swollen, and every time she moved they rubbed against her clothing. She hated sitting down. She still felt like she was sitting on an egg.

'Your arousal is beautiful to us Morgan. To me. On our world, the closer a woman is to seae-bereth, the closer she is to the goddess.'

'But Jyn. I can't live being constantly aroused. To only find relief when I sleep.'

'After the wedding ceremony, your desire will lessen. It won't fully leave you, but you will begin to see it as an old friend. Come here, loved one.'

Jyn called Morgan to his seat and told her to remain standing. He lifted her robe around her waist and was surprised to see that she had grown tiny folds. They were swollen and glistening. He began to firmly lick them and use his fingers inside of her. She was delicious, and she could feel her emotions calming down. Then she climbed on top of him so his -seye could have access to her. She sat firmly on Jyn's lap which set his own desire on fire. Then his -seye began his own work, thrusting and throbbing hard within her.

'Is that better my loved one?'

'Yes. Much better. But I'm tired, Jyn.'

'I know.'

ONCE AGAIN MORGAN WAS resting after Jyn left for the dojo. Jyn told her that her Attendant's mind has been resting on her quite a bit and his desire was growing. She asked him if that was normal.

'Yes. Of course it is Morgan. Your scent envelopes him whenever he is in your presence. There is a part of him that only you can satisfy. He needs to release his seed into you again. I know you are not losing interest in him. Relax and enjoy his Guardianship. He'll be here soon after I leave. Allow yourself to partake of his sacrament while I'm gone.'

She snuggled into the covers and allowed her eyes to close. She kept thinking about the first time she was with him. Not even knowing his name. How beautiful he is. How calming. But it's as if the memory of him fades as soon as he leaves. Jyn told her that was as it should be. Attendants are not lovers or husbands or consorts. They guard the spirit. Keep it centered. They are not meant to be with anyone other than their spouses and their charge. '*It is his duty to fill you spiritually*', he said. 'And *he will know exactly how to do that.*'

She was just drifting off in that thought when she heard him come in. She wondered what it would be like if he just took her. Ravished her. He's always been so careful.

Before she could finish that thought, he was on her like a cat rolling her on her stomach and pushing himself into her. He bent down and hissed in her ear. It was wonderful, and the feeling of submitting to him was different. It wasn't painful, and she found herself more open than she expected. His thrusts were deep and hot and when he came, once again, she absorbed it all. Then he turned her over and bent his mouth to her, hungrily licking her, and initiating the seae-bereth.

She was still throbbing when she woke up. She still desired him. He had drawn her bath and he came in, lifted her from the bed and placed her in the tub. Then he joined her. He began to kiss her deeply and she was so hungry for his kisses, they were so precious and lovely. And his fingers found her again and she lost herself in time.

The whole time, he said nothing but a few whispered prayers. She knew she wouldn't be able to be without him. He looked at her and favored her with the gentlest smile. Then he got out of the tub and helped her out. He dried her off and took her back to bed.

After he was done making love to her, he whispered his name in her ear. '*I am Vek-Seye. And I will be your Guardian forever.*'

CHAPTER TWELVE

MORGAN FELT BETTER the next day. They would be arriving to Prymiah tomorrow, so Jyn and Elrek were meeting to prepare. They would be gone for a while. Vek had been in earlier to give her the morning bath and mercifully that was all it was. He knew she was better, and his job was done for now. She had just finished speaking with Bruce and Idra who were busy planning the finishing touches of the wedding. When she finished the communique with them she remembered how flushed Idra looked and how coy her husband looked. Morgan knew that look. He has been fucking her breathless. The thought made her chuckle. She was glad she wasn't the only one with a wet and swollen pussy.

Lindsey was arriving for breakfast soon and then they would be able to just enjoy each other's company without any men around, Prymiahn or otherwise. It would be lovely.

Lindsey was so glad to see Morgan. Things between her and Alex had been going so well since their time on the ship. And she wanted to thank her mother in law for everything that she and Jyn had done for them. She was amazed at how beautiful Morgan looked. But the sound of her voice was the same. Still soothing and comforting, with a deep wisdom.

They sat comfortably in a private area with deep luxurious seating and a huge alcove that opened up to one of the ship's gardens. Morgan missed Lindsey. Lindsey was the only other human female on Prymiah and seeing her now brought her great joy with a tinge of sadness.

'It's so good to see you, mom. I've missed you. But I want to hear what it's like to have so many husbands. It sounds complicated.'

'Well, I was wondering when you would get to that. You are as curious as I am. Why did you wait?'

'I was embarrassed to be so nosey. But since being on the ship, it seems I am hungry to know it all.'

'Okay, well there are really three types of Prymiahn men. Princes start as warriors, but they are naturally attracted to diplomacy and politics. Jyn is a

Prince. Warriors enjoy the fight and even after missions, they stay in the dojos sparring and competing. Elrek is a Warrior. Priests are...'

Morgan trailed off; she had no idea how to describe Vek.

'And the priests?'

Morgan continued to think about her experiences with her Attendant, and she flushed. Lindsey noticed, and it excited her.

'Priests are a different breed altogether. They are born into priesthood, but they still train as Warriors when they come of age. And then they train to be Guardians, which is part of a holy sect. Priests study the sexual and healing arts.'

'Wow. I can't imagine what it must be like. They are all so sensual.'

'Yes, that's the purpose of this world, after all. But you want to know what it's like to make love with them, even though you won't ask me outright.'

Lindsey nodded.

'Being with Jyn is like being in a fairy tale. He is a Prince, so he carries himself like one. He demands respect, but he understands the weight of his power. Elrek is a Warrior, so I always feel safe with him. But that's not what you want to know, is it?'

'Well, mom. I want to know what it is like to *be* with them. What it's like to share a bed with them.'

She blushed deeply, but Morgan just smiled. It took her a long time to get used to it herself.

'Oh honey, it's fine. It's good to be curious.'

'I just want to know what to expect with Mandy. I think she will want a Prymiah boy. Terrans will be boring to her now.'

'Well. Not necessarily. Bruce still makes my toes curl. He still knows how to scratch my itch. And hopefully little Mandy will experience both-but not too soon. But let's see. Making love with Jyn is all encompassing. He wants to know all of me, so he tests my limits. He is the one that I enjoy when I want to be ravished. He's devilish, but he knows to approach me with respect. He knows how to read me, too. The deepest parts. The parts that enjoy pain play. He hisses when he plays with me. It makes me shiver. He is also very tender with me after. Making sure I have my healing baths. And afterward, I definitely need them.

'Elrek is a very powerful lover, but because of his size, he is extremely gentle. His foreplay can sometimes last hours. When he's done, my desire is so overwhelming, I can barely breathe. He is very pensive, but his hunger for me is palpable. He doesn't usually hiss. But he has a low grumbling growl. He enjoys exploring every inch of me, seeing what makes me flutter. He won't quit until I have multiple orgasms, and he is quite protective. Even more so than Jyn.'

'What do you know about the Priests?'

'Yes. My personal Attendant is a Priest.'

Morgan paused. She enjoys her time with the Attendant. She has only been with him a few times, and each time is more intense.

'Mom?'

'Yes. I have had some experience. Priests are in a class by themselves. When they have you, they have your spirit as well as your body. He acts according to what my sexual spirit needs. It is different each time. More intense. Never painful. And he always pushes me into a deep sleep after. I barely remember what happened until I see him again. It's weird. And I don't desire him unless I need to. I saw him this morning and did not desire him at all. So he only bathed me and left. It was nice actually. I never feel compelled with him. But sometimes, I hunger for him. And when I do, he fills my need.'

'Mom. I...'

'No Lindsey. You don't. You think you do. When I first experienced Jyn-the afternoon he and Kilra arrived-I had no idea what was about to happen to me. Their symbiote's are very large, as you have seen. First, I felt that I was not totally in control of my will. I realized what was happening, but absolutely too relaxed to be normal in the situation I was in. I was repulsed at the sight of the symbiote. Thick, slick, and long, with an actual mouth. It hurt, Lindsey. It hurt quite a bit when Jyn pushed it inside of me. And it was very slow. But as he pushed in, whenever I felt pain, a wave of orgasm hit me. So with each inch that I submitted, I had an orgasm. When he was finally all the way in, the symbiote started to undulate and throb. The pleasure was so intense that I fainted. When I woke up it was as if I had awakened from a dream. But he reminded me that it wasn't a dream and when I finally came to myself, I could feel this throbbing need. From that moment on, I have been open. Anticipating the symbiotes being inside of me. Desire and arousal are my constant companions now. And it's not even just a physical openness that women feel-which is normal during intimacy. I mean my body's seemingly constant willingness to submit. Just the sight of symbiotes arouse me. Makes me hungry for them. And with Elrek, I feel lost. He carries me so far into pleasure, I think my heart is going to explode. Lindsey, I submitted to their ways with a purpose, But my nerves are always on fire. My body spasms are so strong from my own orgasms that I must have healing baths in the mornings, or my muscles would ache all day. My Attendant-the priest-enables me to go into a deep sleep, so I can get true rest. Jyn says when we arrive to home world, I will not feel like this. I can only pray that I don't.'

'But doesn't the priest make love to you too?'

'Yes. But it is to soothe me. It is for me alone. His only desire is to serve my spiritual need. When he ejaculates, I absorb it. It helps me heal. Then he allows me to sleep. If he feels I will still need him after, he stays until I awaken, and takes care of me again.'

'I'm still jealous. Less now, after hearing the misery you are in. But truth be told, Alex is taking care of business in such a way now, that he is not like he ever was before. It is like I have a new husband. It's wonderful.'

'Good. I am so relieved. If Jyn and Elrek thought he was still hurting you, they would cut him to bits.'

The both laughed at this, but they also knew it was true. Lindsey said:

'Why did you hesitate when I asked about your priest Attendant? You didn't even tell me his name.'

'His name is not to be known by anyone but his wife, and now me. He released it to me while he was still inside of me. It was an experience I will never forget. It was if hearing him speak his sacred name did something inside of me that I still don't understand. I guess I hesitated because my need for him is different. He's like a dream that you yearn for but when you have it, you forget it as soon as you awaken.'

Afterward, Lindsey snuggled up to Morgan and fell asleep. She hadn't done that in so long, and Morgan forgot how much she enjoyed stroking Lindsey's hair while she slept. Then she fell asleep herself, in complete comfort and peace-without the slightest help from her Attendant.

But Vek, who was connected to Morgan even more deeply than she realized, felt her peace and the peace of her daughter in law, and thanked the goddess for answering his prayers.

CHAPTER THIRTEEN

ALEX WAS RELIEVED WHEN they arrived to Prymiahn space. He was looking forward to getting off the ship and planting his feet on solid ground. He didn't care what planet he was on. Space travel wasn't for him. He was also thankful that he and his family had their own residence and that the Prymiahns had fitted it with an atmosphere similar to the one on Earth, so he would feel more comfortable.

After he had been there a couple of weeks and the wedding was about to be held, he found himself thinking about everything that had happened and he got antsy, like he had lost his balance on a very high beam. Lindsey had been keeping an eye on him and was starting to get worried.

'Alex, is there something I can do? What is it?'

'It's too much Lindsey. My mind keeps going back to what happened to us and where we are now. I feel like I'm losing my mind-or like I'm in some kind of fucked up nightmare.'

The door chimed.

'Hello, Alex. Lindsey.' Alex said:

'Elrek. What do you want? It's like you people can smell our feelings.'

'Not quite. Lindsey do you mind if Alex and I take a walk? We'll only be gone a couple of hours.'

'No problem, Elrek. I think Alex needs some air.'

She winked at Elrek.

'You're not helping, Lindsey. Anyway, it's just you, right Elrek? That old tomcat's not with you is he?'

'No, Alex. It'll just be us.'

Alex hated being out of his house. At least at home he felt like he was on Earth. But when he walked outside he immediately felt lighter. Too light. Like he was going to float off the ground. But his feet felt heavy. Like nothing could knock him off balance. He felt like a bull in a China shop-one small move, and he would break something. And everything had a slight aura to it. It wasn't too obvious, it was barely there, but it was enough to make everything, and everyone look like they were softly backlit by candlelight.

'Elrek. This place is-beautiful.'

It was the first time Elrek heard Alex say anything positive about his world. He knew he was sincere.

'Thank you Alex. It pleases me you think so. But I sense you are disturbed.'

'Yeah. You could say that. I just feel like none of this is real. Like my mind is being taken over, or that I'm going crazy.'

'Well. We stopped influencing your mind before you left Earth, so no, your mind is not being taken over. And you are definitely not going crazy. I thought you may be out of sorts though, and I thought a long walk would do you good. Have you noticed something?'

'What do you mean?'

'We have been walking for quite a while now. And not only that, but you have also been in the presence of my people-male and female, and...'

'I don't feel aroused!'

'Yes. See? I told you that it would be different when you arrive here. Everyone handles their own affairs, just like you do on Earth.'

'I thought you people worshipped sex.'

'No, Alex. We worship the planet goddess, Prymiah. Intimacy is our sacrament to her. But we believe in balance above all. There is a time and place for all things. Here we are.'

Alex could barely see the doorway. It looked almost disguised in a cluster of lush greenery.

'Come in Alex, this is the main Dojo.'

'Now this, I understand.'

'I thought you might. Look around. You will not only train with me, but with you father and your half-brothers. We will hold expedition matches here. All Vok-tor acolytes do.'

'Acolytes?'

'Yes. As the Revered Mother's son, you must be trained to be a Temple Warrior.'

'Oh hell no, Elrek. Nope. Sounds like not happening.'

'Listen, Alex. Temple Warriors are some of the strongest of us. Just under the Temple Guardians. We stand with the captains in battle. If the planet comes under siege, we surround the temple to take care of our precious artifacts. And more than that-we are charged with protecting the Revered Mother.'

'You said *we*. Are you a temple warrior?'

'Yes. And you, your brothers, and your father will be as well. It is a great honor. But you must train harder than most.'

'Don't tell me. My Terran blood, right?'

'Not quite the whole story. You will have a harder time maintaining balance, true. But not only because of your Terran blood. You have Prymiahn blood coursing through your veins.'

'Elrek. Just because I am here does not mean I have Prymiahn blood now.'

'Of course not. But your mother does. Your grandmother was half-Prymiahn.'

Alex looked like he was struck by lightning. He stood there motionless. To him it felt like time had stopped. Elrek told him the story that Morgan would be told after her wedding.

'Elrek. All this time. Some things I have questioned about my life makes sense now. My temper. My passions. Elrek. My sweet girl Mandy. Oh no.'

'It is as it should be Alex. And Mandy will be fine. She is where she needs to be for now. But she is a daughter of Earth and will return there. But your mother will be the highest member of the council now. And a symbol of our faith. And as such, she will need those around her to be prepared to defend her to the death. And another thing Alex. Your mother does not know yet that she has Prymiahn blood and will not be told until after the wedding.'

'Why would you keep something like that from my mom?'

'Because she needs to remain calm until after the ceremony. She is unsettled and if she finds out beforehand...'

'Mom is going to be pissed off.'

Alex began to laugh.

'What is so funny, Alex?'

'She's gonna try to kill you motherfuckers!'

BEFORE THE WEDDING took place, Bruce had arranged to stay with Alex and his family. There was more than enough room for multiple households. And because he looked after the twins with Idra while waiting for Morgan's transport to arrive, he had grown attached to them. He practically took them everywhere and they cried when he left to go anywhere without them. But he changed their names. He absolutely hated the Prymiahn ones and Morgan finally relented. He called the one that looked like Morgan, Johnathan and the other one, David.

When the transport arrived, He knew Morgan would be whisked off to be prepared for the wedding, so he got to help Alex and Lindsey finish unpacking. He was overjoyed to see his granddaughter Mandy, and she greeted him with a loud 'GRANDY!!!' and ran to hug his legs. She took to the twins immediately and kept them within her eyesight. But Lindsey had already laid a huge quilt in the middle of the floor and got down on it with all the babies and just basked in their joy. She then informed Bruce and Alex that they could help the Attendants with the boxes, since she had her hands full. This gave Bruce and Alex time to get reacquainted.

'Dad, it'll be great to have you here. I missed you. But you have a Prymiahn residence too, don't you?'

'Yes. But I think I've spent enough time with them. Idra is a lovely woman and I care for her deeply. But she is not your mother. I'm hoping Morgan will spend time here, too.'

'Me too. I don't see it, to be honest, dad. She seems so caught up.'

'Part of her is. Just like part of me was. But I'm going to visit her after the wedding and before she starts training.'

Alex saw something in his dad's eyes he hadn't seen in a while. Cunning. And he also knew enough to keep his thoughts about the matter to himself. Bruce said:

'We'll get to hunt here. The Prymiahns have a game preserve that allows hunters to stalk prey to get meat. There are a few dozen varieties of prey and as long as we eat what we kill, they allow it. I went out with this fellow named Mik-I think he's one of the Admirals of the fleet-anyway, the prey is challenging to hunt, and they hunt with bow and arrow-our favorite. We can teach the twins.'

'Wow. I can't wait. It's been a while since I've been bow-hunting. But I heard we both have to continue Vok-tor training-at least 3 hours per day.'

'Yep. While you were training on the ship, I was training here. I like it, to be honest. Kilra has been training me, and she is hard core. But she's been called away on mission, so Elrek will be training us both, it seems.'

'Dang, dad. Elrek is like some kind of Vok-tor guru. He's gonna try to kill us.'

'I've heard. Your mom has it worse I think.'

'Why is that?'

'Varek is going to train her. He's the Supreme High Priest. I heard he is worse than Elrek when it comes to training.'

'Mom is stubborn. He's gonna piss her off.'

'No doubt, Alex. But she has to learn to fight, too. She has to defend herself. She's all spit and fire when she's mad, and she'll cut you just for fun. But she's not disciplined. Not the way she needs to be.'

'Don't let her hear you say that. Mom is fierce. I think you are too. You remind me today of how you were when I was a little kid. I was scared of you. But I would fight anybody that said something about my dad. When will Elrek train us?'

'About three weeks from now. After the wedding.'

'That's not a lot of time for your honeymoon.'

'There's gonna be more time than you think, son.'

Alex saw that cunning look on his dad's face again, and it made him smile. That was the man that could stalk prey miles into the woods without making a sound. The man with a hot temper but a fierce devotion to his family. This was the man who was in the Navy and later the one in law enforcement that took a bullet in the chest to save his captain and then drove both of them to the hospital. Yeah. He saw a flash of something go across his dad's face. He got almost giddy thinking about what was going on in his dad's mind.

Then Lindsey called out that they had had enough time to chit-chat. She and the babies were hungry.

Then he heard Mandy say:

'Yep daddy! We're hungry!'

Alex thought to himself that all the women in his life told him what to do. But he wouldn't have it any other way.

CHAPTER FOURTEEN

MORGAN HAD ALREADY been warned that weddings are taken very seriously on Prymiah.

Two days before the ceremony she was sequestered in a spacious area away from everyone but her Attendant Vek-Seye and occasionally his wife, Ysa. She was required to fast until after the ceremony because they wanted her to be mentally sharp and focused. She was to drink a preparation that emptied her bowels, and she could swear that it tasted like the prep she had to drink before having a colonoscopy. Afterward she could only have water. It suited her fine because she had absolutely no appetite whatsoever.

The first evening she was groomed completely. All hair except her eyebrows and what was on her head was completely removed. But they left a bit of hair on her pubic area. Then her skin was exfoliated with a rough cloth. Afterward she was bathed in essential oils and allowed to dry naturally. Vek-Seye was not permitted to touch her in any way except what was required to prepare her for her wedding. After the bath, she was surprised at how relaxed she was. Then Vek allowed her to recline so he could wash her hair in a ceremonial bowl. He massaged her scalp with cleansers that pleasantly tingled. He took his time massaging her scalp and she began to drift off. While she was napping, Vek prepared seating for her so that she would be comfortable whether sitting or reclining. She would not be permitted any books. Soft music played in the background and a soft musky incense permeated the room. Vek said that this was one of the only times he and his wife would be permitted to speak to her openly with others present. He said she should let them know at any time if she needed something. But in the evenings, after he was done serving her, he must sit with his back to her, out of respect but since she had learned how to speak mind to mind, she should do so now if it was more comforting to her.

She was thinking about how lonely she was, and how she missed Earth.

'Morgan, why are you lonely when so much love surrounds you?'

'I miss my home, Vek. I wonder why this has happened to me. Why I let it happen.'

'I see. May I speak freely?'

'Yes, of course.'

'Very well. You hate us as much as you love us. The hate is as it should be. We took your world from you. We changed you, made you a stranger to your family. But you love us as well. Your compassion covers the hate. You love Jyn and Elrek despite what was taken from you. Your feelings-in such opposition to each other- is the perfect example of balance.'

'How do you know this about me, Vek? Those are feelings I would never share with anyone. In fact, I thought they were hidden in my secret place.'

'There are things that only I will know because I serve you as Guardian. I know all of you, Morgan. More than Bruce, Jyn or Elrek. More than yourself. Why are your thoughts drifting to my wife?'

'I can't help it. On my world, all of this would be adulterous, sinful. I can't seem to shake feeling guilty.'

'Prymiah is your world now. Ysa loves serving you as much as I do. She knows the depth of my devotion to you. She knows how far I will go to please you. She would expect nothing less. Your guilt has no place. I know you enjoy our times together. I feel your desire.'

'It is not the same.'

'No. It is not supposed to be. It is deeper. More intense.'

'Why is that?'

'Because you have nothing to hide from me. I guard your spirit, so it trusts me before your mind does. Before your body does. I know that you hide from Bruce the sadness you feel sometimes when you think how easy it was for him to succumb to Kilra, even though logically you know he was no more able to resist her than you were able to resist Jyn. I know you hate the fact that you desire Jyn even though he has been responsible for so much unfamiliar pain. And that you even feel guilty for enjoying that pain. I know that when you are with Elrek, that is the only time you wish you were truly Prymiahn and that he had been your first. I know that your love for him runs deeper than any man you have ever been with. And yes. I know how you enjoy how swollen with lust I make you.'

'Vek. How...?'

'I possess two sentient -seyes. One is more ancient than you know. More sensitive. He has only asserted himself once before and that was before he was implanted in me as a High Priest. The last Revered Mother he bonded with before you, was the first. Jali-seae.'

'Why?'

'Only he knows, and I trust his judgement.'

'I'm so tired Vek.'

'I know. But you have many years to serve and be served. Prymiah needs you, and so does Earth. I will be with you to help you when you are overwhelmed. Even now, my presence is helping you.'

'In what way?'

'Your body yearns for me. I feel you opening up. That is part of my purpose in preparing you for your wedding. Otherwise your thoughts of so many things would prevent you from being totally immersed in the ceremony and its activities.'

'Oh no. I forgot you could feel everything I do.'

'There is no need for shame or embarrassment. Even though I cannot physically touch you, I will be intimate with you. It will be easy for me because I long to be bonded to you again. To be inside you and empty myself into you. As you sleep, you will dream of me inside of you, and it will seem like a memory. It will comfort you.'

Morgan allowed her mind to rest on what Vek revealed to her. Then she giggled because she had cold feet. Not fear of the ceremony, but actual cold feet. Vek spoke:

'Would you like a warm towel for your feet?'

'Yes, Vek. Since it is absolutely impossible for me to keep anything from you. Even the smallest of my desires.'

'You are right. And after a time, but not far from now, I will fill you up in a way you won't expect.'

UNLIKE TERRAN WEDDINGS, the reception happens before the ceremony itself. The guests mingle, eat, drink, and meet with the couples.

There are very few guests, though. Immediate family, of course. And members of the council with their mates.

Bruce was fascinated. He kept looking at Morgan because he knew more than most how uncomfortable she was. She was beautiful of course. She had on a sheer robe with golden prayer verses stitched all over it. She was nude beneath it. Her hair was down and the only jewelry she wore was a pendant the color of a brilliant emerald carried by a golden chain which was fashioned by the Goldsmith. It was nestled between her breasts. She carried a blush on her cheeks that he imagined would be there until this was all over. He caught her eye and she smiled at him. There was so much in that smile. But when he smiled back, he made sure she saw greedy lust for her in his smile, and she must have. She quickly looked away. This pleased Bruce greatly, because when Bruce was with Idra for the first time, he suddenly remembered an aspect of his relationship with Morgan that he had long forgotten. And he intended to remind her soon.

She was unsteady on her feet, which he was told was natural because of her fast before, and her exposure to everyone's desire to be in her presence and enveloped in her pheromones. Because of this, Varek guided her to greet guests very gently, allowing her to rest her arm on his. And he, as High Priest was dressed regally, draped in a dark green overcoat, which covered his own battle regalia. His long white hair pulled up in a tight ponytail that was braided and sitting regally on top of his head.

Jyn and Elrek walked at least six feet behind her and the priest. Side by side. They also had overcoats on. Green for Jyn, who was Varek's brother. And a golden overcoat for Elrek. Both -seyes were exposed, but cuffed by exquisite golden rings, with prayers etched on each. They would be removed for the consummation. Their claws were exposed.

And Bruce was satisfied to see that they, also, looked flushed and uncomfortable.

He himself was sitting next to Idra, his own Prymiahn bride. She was breathtaking. A pure white robe for her, with stitching in green. Her white hair loosened and free. Thankfully, they would be able to enjoy each other in private, although he had to expose himself as well, and he did not enjoy being cuffed. He would catch Idra looking at him, and when he did her breath would quicken just a bit. His would too. He could hardly wait until he could have her.

He glanced at everyone that was there, and he found who he was looking for. Alex and Lindsey. They were mixing well enough. And at least their own clothes were more modest. Alex had refused to be cuffed. But Bruce saw regret on his son's face. This place was full of pheromones. And Alex was obviously aroused. Lindsey, being the good wife that she is, tried to stay in front of him to shield his embarrassment, but Bruce thought it didn't matter one bit. The Prymiahns knew. And they enjoyed it.

So did he. His son was so stubborn sometimes. This would be a long night for Alex.

The ceremony was about to begin.

They were deep in Varek's garden. The moons were full. Everyone was helped to their seats by Attendants who were in place to guard and serve. Each of the Attendants wore the same battle regalia as Varek.

They were beautiful, but lethal.

There was a raised platform at the front. It had two chairs facing each other on either end, and there was an area that had been constructed for Morgan to consummate her marriage to Jyn and Elrek.

It was constructed in the shape of a square. Sheer curtains covered it, but there was another set at the back. The guests were only meant to see the shadow of the couple.

He and Idra were led to sit in the chairs at the front of the platform. They faced each other. These seats were places of high honor, as they were the first spouses of the Revered Mother and her -Shaed. They were to remain perfectly still and only gaze at each other. This was to symbolize their agreement with the union, and to stoke their desire for each other.

Bruce tried not to think about how tight his cuffs were becoming.

Varek then gently escorted Morgan to the inner curtain. He could see Varek slip her robe off, so that Morgan was completely nude. Even her shadow was beautiful. Then Varek moved to face her. He was three feet away and whispering to her quietly. And behind him was a giant bell.

An Attendant than led Jyn to Morgan and left. Varek had already taken his place beside the bell.

The assembly was completely still.

Varek sounded the bell. Once.

Jyn moved to Morgan and held her closely.

The assembly could hear their moans and screams of pleasure, even though they were standing almost perfectly still. The symbiote was doing its work. After Varek was certain the consummation was complete, he sounded the bell twice. Jyn then took his place behind Morgan.

An Attendant then led Elrek to Morgan and left. It was the same as with Jyn, with one exception.

Morgan called out Elrek's name at the end. Elrek then took his place behind Morgan, next to Jyn.

Varek sounded the bell twice.

Then Varek came out of the area and announced to the assembly that the marriages of the Revered Mother have been consummated. He then admonished the assembly to depart and celebrate the blessings of Prymiah.

Bruce could not help but notice the ecstasy on the faces of everyone. Some were crying. But they left quickly. Bruce knew why. It was going to be a noisy night.

After everyone had left, Varek turned to Bruce and Idra. He looked like he was going to fall down. His face looked like he had seen a god. He was sweating.

'Your families have been blessed. There was an abundance of seed. Allow the Attendants to guide you home. Jyn and Elrek will leave with their own Attendants, but Vek must attend to the Revered Mother before she returns to you. You will not see her until the morning. It is as it should be.'

CHAPTER FIFTEEN

VEK HAD STATIONED HIMSELF at the back of the platform to be ready to retrieve the Revered Mother at the end of the ceremony. He allowed himself to be absorbed in all of her feelings. There was such arousal and conflict, and he knew she would be exhausted and physically ill. But in addition, and because of his rank as Guardian, he was allowed to be uncuffed and his own -seyes were able to partake in the pleasure of their brethren by their own psychic link. As each consummation took place, he felt his own -seyes fill with what felt like years of fluid. Right before the ceremony was over, they released copious amounts of seed, much to the relief of Vek.

Before his -seyes retreated, Vek quietly cleaned and cuffed them and drew on his ceremonial robe. He cleaned his hands and face with the anointed cloths that he had prepared beforehand and waited for the bell that would signal his time to approach.

When the bell finally sounded, Vek tentatively approached Morgan, who was standing next to Varek. She looked exhausted. She had been sweating profusely, and her hair was stuck in damp, curly tendrils on her face and shoulders. The sheer robe she wore clung to her body, showing her full breasts and hardened nipples. She was absolutely breathtaking.

Without speaking, Varek slowly walked Morgan over to Vek, allowing him to grasp her hand and lead her down from the platform. They began slowly walking deeper into the garden. After they had been walking for some time Vek said:

'Morgan, we have been walking for quite a few minutes. You haven't spoken. Tell me. How is it with you?'

Morgan stood still, looked up at Vek, and ran to the edge of the path where she started violently dry-heaving. Vek ran to her.

'Morgan. You will be fine. Come. Let's continue. I have a space set up for you where you can sit and have a little water. Then we can speak comfortably.'

Soon, they were even deeper in the garden. The only noises she heard were the nocturnal animals that move swiftly and softly to avoid predators. They finally arrived at a private area that Vek had set up. A soft seat and a table with a chalice and two glasses. Morgan never ceased to be amazed at how the Prymiahns could bring luxury and comfort to any area they occupied. Vek nodded for her to sit.

'Now, Morgan. Sit for a moment. Drink some water. Sip it slowly or you will start to heave again.'

'Vek, why do I feel like I want to die? I feel helpless and weak. I can barely breathe, and I don't want to do anything but sleep.'

'When Prymiahns marry, the -male symbiote enters the female and moves within her until both she and -her husband are at the cusp of orgasm. The symbiotes completely control each host. But the hosts are not allowed to feel the release. The reason for this, is so the symbiotes can absorb all of the sexual energy of the couple. Then after the ceremony, when the couple are alone, they can finally have release. You are miserable because you had to receive the symbiotes of two men. Your body is not ready for that type of activity. That is why you are dehydrated, tired, nauseous, and weak. My purpose is to help you release a portion of your orgasm. But not all of it. The greater portion of pleasure will be for your husbands to give you.'

'Vek. I'm tired. I don't want to have sex. I don't want you right now. I want to sleep.'

'And you will. I will not enter you tonight. My purpose is not to bond with you, but to strengthen you and relieve your misery. I am your Guardian, remember?'

'Yes.'

'Morgan of Earth, Revered Mother of Prymiah, do you trust me?'

'Yes, Vek. You know that I do.'

'Please do as I say just for a little while. And you will feel much better when you awaken. I need you to remove your robe. It is sopping wet, and you are shivering. I will not remove my robes, and you will not see my -seyes. I will sit on the ground, see? And you will lay on the ground with your head in my lap and your eyes focused on the stars. The ground on Prymiah gives off heat and you will feel better.'

'What's going to happen to me, Vek?'

'I will give you a memory. It will be as if you are there, but it is only a memory. You will feel more like yourself after. Then I will push you to sleep and cover you. You will rest until you are ready. And I will know when that is.'

Morgan did as she was told and lay on the ground facing the sky. Vek cradled her head as she lay there, and her breathing slowed. He was right about the ground. It was warm and inviting, and soon she found herself falling asleep and having a dream she did not expect.

After Vek returned Morgan to her home, Varek met him outside.

'How was it with her, Vek?'

'She will be ready for you in the morning, Varek.'

'Did you give her the memory?'

'Yes.'

'Did she receive it?'

'Yes. She was pleased that it was me who comforted her when her husband strayed. She didn't seem surprised, and her knowledge of it enhanced her release. She is quite ready for what awaits her. From you and from her husbands.'

'Good. It is as it should be.'

WHEN MORGAN AWAKENED, she was startled to find Jyn lying next to her, looking at her lovingly.

'I was dreaming that I was snuggled between you and Elrek.' Jyn said:

'It wasn't a dream. Vek carried you home and placed you in bed. You were so exhausted after the ceremony. Elrek and I climbed in on either side of you and slept ourselves. It would seem each of our -seyes wanted you to themselves at the ceremony. It was... difficult. It is as it should be.'

'Where is Elrek?'

'You will see him later. I have something to discuss with you.'

'You sound serious, Jyn. And I don't like that I can't catch any of your thoughts.'

'Morgan.'

Jyn sighed. He dreaded the conversation he must have.

'Morgan. You were always meant to share my bed. And Prymiah has always been your home.'

'What are saying, Jyn?'

'Your grandmother was raped by one of our scouts. Your mother carried our bloodlines. And because our genes are dominant, she would have been more Prymiahn than Terran.'

'Jyn?!'

'Please let me finish. We knew she suffered from our traits without understanding why. But we were not given permission to take Earth, so we had to leave her in her suffering. But we watched you because we knew that if you could tolerate our blood, that you would be ready by the time Earth was made a protectorate.'

By now Morgan was pacing the floor. Tears were streaming down her face. She said in hitching whispers:

'My dad had mom committed briefly. He said she had been acting out of sorts and he could no longer control her. I found out later that she had taken to the streets, selling herself. Finally her doctors put her on heavy anti-depressants and released her to dad's care. After dad died, I went to see her, and I heard her sobbing in their bedroom. I thought it was grief. When I went to look in on her she was face-down, sobbing on the floor and asking God why he created her, and why did she have to suffer like this. When I went in to soothe her, she stopped crying and she told me about why she was committed. She said it was her sex drive. She couldn't help it. She said she drove dad mad with it, and when he couldn't satisfy her, she took to the streets. She even apologized for what she had that doctor do to me years ago. She thought it would keep me from the uncontrolled desire she suffered with. A few months after that conversation she was dead. She had killed herself.'

'Morgan, I am so sorry.'

'But that's not true is it? You bastards killed my mother! She had no idea what was happening to her, and you left her to suffer. And look at me! All those years. I have no idea how I survived. I guess I was just too stubborn.'

She strode to Jyn and slapped him hard across the face, leaving a scratch.

Jyn did not move except to grasp her shoulders gently. He looked deep into her eyes.

'You were stronger, Morgan.'

'Strong? Strong? Nothing kept me but my faith. Nothing! I still pray, you know. Despite loving you and loving Elrek, I pray. Despite breaking Bruce's heart and betraying my family, I pray. I prayed when you ravished me and when

I enjoyed it. I asked forgiveness for my desire while submitting to it. Even now, I love you and hate you more than I ever have. You bastards. You started with my grandmother...'

'But it ends with you, loved one. We know what we have done to your family. You are here not only because you are Prymiah's daughter. You are here because of your resilience. Your strength. You say it comes from your god. I cannot deny you your faith any more than you can deny us ours. To us it doesn't matter. You are ours and we love you. Most of our people want to stop the forced colonizations because the whole of Prymiah has watched you from birth and loved you. This is your homecoming.'

Morgan fell to her knees and sobbed. Jyn caught her and sat on the floor with her. She slapped him hard across his face again, but he stayed with her and eventually she allowed herself to lean into his embrace. Jyn said:

'Morgan, when I first heard of the mission to retrieve you, I was ambitious and wanted it. I watched you from afar from when you were a child and I lusted for you when you were a young woman. But when Elrek finally scouted for you and showed me who you had become, my feelings for you deepened quickly and I fell in love. In my arrogance I thought I would seduce you, but you gave of yourself so freely, my heart melted, and I was yours before you ever became mine.'

'I want to kill you, Jyn. I want to cut your throat.'

Jyn chuckled.

'Why the hell is that funny?'

'Because as a Prymiahn female, I would expect nothing less.'

AFTER HER TALK WITH Jyn, Morgan left the bedroom to walk around her new home. Palace was more like it. It just made her tired. So she went back to her chamber and found a plump couch to sit in. Everywhere she looked she could see gardens. It was gorgeous. But she had started to cry again when Elrek walked in. He sat carefully next to her. Her shoulders slumped. This saddened him greatly.

'Loved one, I see you have spoken with Jyn.'

'Yes. I'm overwhelmed with anger and grief. My mom and dad suffered so much without knowing why. And I am reaping the benefit of their suffering.'

'Morgan, I cannot disagree. And you are not going to like what I have to say, either.'

'What is this? You both are tag-teaming me now?'

'No. Well, yes in a way. We want to share your emotions regardless of what they are. So we thought to speak with you in such a manner.'

'Well, get on with it, Elrek. I'm just about done.'

'Jyn told you about your origin and why you arrived to be here. Now that you are here, you represent a great power to our world, and by extension, all of its protectorates.'

'Elrek, I know I'm considered the Revered Mother of *this* planet.'

'No. You are the Revered Mother of this planet and *every* planet under our protection.'

'Elrek, I love you, but I swear I'm going to murder you and Jyn in your sleep.'

Elrek laughed.

'Well, I guess I'd better get it all out before it's too late. Not only that, but you are also considered the High Priestess and religious leader of our world. You will serve as the head of our priesthood.'

'No. No I'm not. This is impossible on so many levels.'

'It may feel impossible, but nevertheless, it is so. It is as it should be.'

'If you say, *'it is as it should be'* one more time to my face, I will cut your ponytail off.'

'Morgan, please. It is... imperative that you understand your role. Varek will be here in the morning to take you to the temple.'

'Is that all?'

'No.'

'Where is my blade? That ponytail is not all I'm going to cut off.'

'As High Priestess you are head of the Council now. But you will be training for quite some time, and it will be a while before you take your position. All but one of the council members agree, but that will be discussed sometime later.'

'Well Elrek, I think you can just decline on my behalf. '

'That is not our way.'

'Are you finished? Is Jyn? Who else is coming to give me bad news? Will it be Idra? Kiisma? I trusted you all!'

'And you still can. Can you imagine if we told you all of this while you were on Earth? We would have had to put you in stasis until you arrived home.'

Morgan began to cry again. Then in a rage she got up, found a heavy object, and threw it at Elrek, hitting him square in the chest. He caught his breath and started laughing. This just made Morgan even more frustrated, and she picked up something else and was about to throw it, when Elrek pounced on her quicker than a cat. He looked her straight in the eye.

'My wife. That's enough. Your anger excites me, but I cannot have you until you have been trained at the temple for some time. But if you try to hurt me again, I will remind you how miserable with desire I can make you and of that you may be certain. Then you won't be angry because your thoughts will be elsewhere. Do you understand that as much as Jyn and I desire you, we respect you first as our High Priestess and second as our wife? You must be allowed to be yourself and feel your true emotions without our interference.'

Morgan stood quietly. There was nothing else to do. She had not noticed that Vek was standing in the doorway.

'See Morgan? Your Guardian is here to make sure I behave.'

When she saw Vek, she immediately felt better. She couldn't understand why. Just his presence calmed her down. But she felt defeated.

'Vek must speak with you before you leave for the temple. I am quite jealous. Since the wedding last night, he has seen more of you than any of your husbands. Be assured that when you are ready to receive us, you will need healing baths for a week.'

Vek hissed. It startled Morgan, as it was the first time she had ever heard him hiss that loudly. His canines were bared. Then he said:

'That is quite enough, my -Shaed. Leave her to me. As you know, she is in the care of her Temple Guardian now, and I will meet her needs.'

Elrek hissed back, but he was smiling.

'Yes, Guardian. Of this I am certain. It is as it should be.'

CHAPTER SIXTEEN

AFTER VEK PRESENTED Morgan to Varek, he took her in hand.

'We are going into a deeper part of my garden for a moment, Morgan. You seem apprehensive.'

'A little. Varek, I feel like my world is spinning out of control. Nothing I assumed about Prymiah is true, but at the same time, it feels familiar. I guess I know why that is now.'

'Yes. You feel out of balance. You are a daughter of two worlds. Not only that, but the energy is also different here. Is it not?'

'Yes. It seems calmer. When I was on Earth with you, everything seemed so frenzied, so passionate. I thought it would be similar here. But I find it more relaxed than I expected. '

'How do you feel about that?'

'Relief.'

'Yes. We are not focused on colonization. So we only release normal amounts of pheromones. And you don't feel us in your mind now, do you?'

'No. Why is that?

'As the Revered Mother, none but your husbands and Guardian may dwell there. Even I may only catch your surface thoughts. I cannot intrude unless you allow me. And here, your Prymiahn blood is dominant. So there is no need to harness you.'

'Harness?'

'Yes. On Earth, your thoughts were in conflict with each other. You may have refused to come home. We couldn't allow this.'

Morgan's shoulders slumped.

'Does this make you angry?'

'Yes. But not something I didn't expect. But I feel something else I can't quite describe.'

'You feel safe.'

'Yes!'

'Our world is one of balance. So as a female, you have as much power as a male. More so in your position. Our planet demands it. Some things we say would have different meanings on Earth. After you have trained with me for a time, you will receive your husbands again.'

'I was told.'

'They will finish you.'

'What? Am I to be a human sacrifice now? Why are you smiling? I'm serious, Varek.'

'I know you are. But remember what I just said. Words have different meanings here. A husband must finish his wife after their wedding. That means that he must allow her to finish reaching her ultimate climax, and that task is his and his alone. He must sacrifice all of himself to you in order to reach his goal. And once that has occurred, you will know it, because you will not be the same.'

'That doesn't sound balanced. What about his pleasure?'

'Well, unlike on Earth, a husband is not worthy of his wife until he can finish her. To do that he must move between your Savage heart and your Saintly one. And it will not be predictable. A woman's desire may change moment to moment. Once you are finished, then you will be more liberated to share your own gifts with them. You will be the one to finish your husbands.'

'What are you not telling me?'

'You are the first Revered Mother with two -Shaeds.'

'Well, yes. I understood that when I was bound to Elrek.'

'Your husbands will be in competition with each other to find who will finish you best.'

'Oh brother. Still with this.'

'Yes. So, I will be more insistent with my training. Both physical and mental.'

'There is something else, isn't there?'

'Yes. Your Guardian will be there each time.'

'Vek? Why?'

'The memory he gave you last night. Do you remember it?'

'Of course. I was pleased that he has been with me all along.'

'He didn't show you the entire memory.'

'Why?'

'Do you remember how centered you felt after? How much at peace? So much so that you were able to easily forgive Bruce for his indiscretion?'

'Yes. It was amazing. I thought no more about it, and if my heart felt broken again, I would have another dream.'

'Yes. The reason why Vek will be there is because he was the first to finish you. You were not permitted to remember it because it was a spiritual act and because...'

'I never would have been satisfied by Bruce after.'

'Yes. So he will observe your coupling with both Jyn and Elrek.'

'Oh. Oh no Varek. Will he...?'

'Yes. If either of them fail you, he will mount you himself and finish you. He knows how more than any man. Even Elrek. He mended your broken heart. He was with you every time it was broken. And after you were married, he requested to be your Guardian, and the council agreed. His position is one of high honor and he takes it seriously. He will not see you displeased.'

'What would happen to Jyn or Elrek then?'

'Vek will kill the one who displeases you and take his place as your -Shaed.'

Morgan looked even more tired than before.

'Varek. Why are we going deeper into your garden. It seems to be getting darker in this part.'

'It is. You will come here twice. Today, and again after your initial training. It is a secret place, wild and unpredictable. You are the first off-worlder to see it. And only Elrek, Vek, and I spend time here.'

'It's too quiet. Its early in the morning and it feels like midnight in here.'

'Are you afraid?'

'Yes.'

'Good. I cannot predict what will happen. I am taking you to meet your relatives.'

'Observe, Morgan.'

As Morgan's eyes adjusted to the darkness, she noticed that right in front of her was a large area of wet ground. Gradually, a soft glow began to surface, and then to her horror, she saw them.

Large, pale serpents, writhing among each other. She could hear the slickness of their movements. They filled her with dread. These were the serpents from her adolescent dream.

'No. Varek.'

'Why are you frightened? These are the Ancient Ones. The brothers and sisters of the same -seyes that you welcomed within your being and grew to love. They have already loved you, even before you knew we existed.'

'Varek. They are dangerous.'

'No, my child. They are wild. They are without boundaries. They want to feel you. They want to know that you belong to them now. They want to know that they belong to you.'

Morgan noticed that the ground beneath her feet was getting softer, more wet, warmer. She had a pit in her stomach. But something else stirred in her too.

'Come. I will lead you to them. They will not harm you. It will be different from your dream. You will see.'

'Don't leave me, Varek.'

'I will lead you to them, but I must not stay with you while you commune with them. It is personal. Intimate. But I will be waiting for you just outside of the nest when they are done.'

Varek led Morgan deeper into the nest. With each step she took, she sunk deeper into the ground. She began to feel them slide over her feet.

'Lay down, Morgan.'

'Varek.'

'Do as I say, child. Lay down with your ancestors.'

Morgan slowly reclined on what was left of the ground. She felt them at her back, cushioning her. They were warm and wet, and her skin tingled as they touched her. Then they began to crawl over her, and she started to struggle but when she did she began to hear them whispering. No, she *felt* them whispering in a language she shouldn't have understood but did. She closed her eyes. She felt them strip off her clothing with their insistent movements. And the whispers became louder in her mind. They explored every part of her, but what they explored more, was her mind. She saw things she did not understand. Things about the galaxy they live in, the fluidity of time, the wonderful feeling of exploration. The exchange of knowledge that is more addictive than any other experience. And as she fell asleep, she felt her own wetness mingle with theirs.

When she awoke, she was laying on the warm ground, Varek had dressed her in a warm covering and was sitting next to her with a glass of water for her to sip. The Ancestors were nowhere to be seen.

Now that you have been with the Ancestors, Morgan, do you have a greater understanding?

'Somewhat. They needed me to know that the passion they seek is not from physical intimacy as much as the acquisition of knowledge, that my curiosity is a blessing to them.'

'Yes. Are you still afraid of them?'

'Yes.'

'Why?'

'They are powerful, Varek. And they draw that power from something even deeper and more powerful than themselves. A power that was ancient on this world before they were created. I could get lost in seeking that power, Varek. So yes, I am afraid.'

'Good. It is as it should be. And you will learn more as I train you. Then you will visit them again.'

CHAPTER SEVENTEEN

RIGHT AFTER MORGAN'S transport arrived, Bruce asked to speak with Varek privately.

'Bruce, it's good to see you after so long. But I see you have an urgent matter to discuss.'

'Yes, Varek. I will see Morgan after Vek brings her to you, and before her training.'

Both men remained silent. Bruce opened up his mind to Varek.

'I see.'

Not much had surprised Varek in his 600 years. But this did. He was intrigued.

'How much time will you need?'

Bruce, seeing the knowing smile on Varek's face, said:

'Two hours will be fine. But if I need to stay longer, I will.'

'You may certainly see your wife, Bruce. I will not interfere. It is as it should be.'

'Not yet, Varek. But it will be.'

BRUCE MET MORGAN AT a grocery store. He was shopping to get some grapes and when he looked up, he saw her. But not really. He saw Morgan's hair. Thick and curly, almost covering her face because she had a cantaloupe right up on her nose smelling its navel deeply. Then she caressed its skin, put it down and picked up another one. This made him smile. He slowly walked up to her to ask what she was doing. She didn't seem a bit taken aback by the approach of some strange man.

'Excuse me. May I ask why you are molesting this poor cantaloupe?'

Morgan, liking the energy of this man looked up at him and gave Bruce a smile that caused him to immediately think of the things he would do to that mouth. Then he realized. He knew her.

'Well. You can't really tell if a fruit like cantaloupe is ready to eat until you pick it up and smell it at the navel. If you smell sweetness and earth, it will be delicious. But you also have to feel the texture of it. If it gives, just a bit, it's ripe enough. But if it's hard and firm, it needs to sit for a day or two on your counter, then its ready.'

Morgan then took Bruce's hand and guided it over the flesh of the cantaloupe. Her hand was soft and gentle, and she used her fingertips to brush the back of his hand ever-so-subtly. He trembled.

'See? This one-even though it smells ripe, is too hard.'

Bruce was also getting too hard.

'Now smell it. Breath in deeply. Do you see what I said about earth and sweetness?'

Surprisingly, he did. She said:

'This one's a keeper.'

Bruce, not one to miss an opportunity said:

'I've learned something today. I think I could use more lessons. How about we get together for a coffee sometime. And go over all the different ways fruit can be handled.'

Morgan had noticed an older lady looking at the tomatoes and eavesdropping on their conversation. When Morgan looked up at her, she smiled, giving Morgan a secret nod and wink.

'I'd love to have coffee with you. You look like a man who's willing to learn a few things about fruit.'

Bruce chuckled in a way that sent shivers down Morgan's spine.

After they had exchanged numbers, Morgan watched as he left the produce section with a bag of grapes. She couldn't help noticing how yummy his rear view was, and it pleased her a bit too much to see him very carefully adjust himself as he was walking off.

'That's a good sign.' She thought to herself.

And as Bruce gathered himself, he realized where he knew her from. They were in high school together. She was his secret crush. Maybe this time, it wouldn't need to be kept a secret.

When Bruce and Morgan were dating, he was pleasantly surprised at how spontaneous she was in bed. She loved trying new things and that suited him because there were times he liked to play a bit rough. She enjoyed how he would stalk her when she got home from work or shopping, just like a predator, and once he caught her, force her against a wall, or over a counter, and even chasing her through his back field only to strip her when he caught her and fuck her raw. Oh how wet she was. Full of desire and wild. And not only that, when most of his past lovers couldn't handle his size, Morgan relished in his dick and took it all in. But the one thing Bruce would not do-*could* not do-is engage Morgan in pain play. She tried to get him to try it, but he would only consent to a rough spanking every now and then-and not one that left a mark. She was too precious to him, and when he asked why she wanted to try it, she just sighed and told him never mind.

And she was always pensive after their play time, even if it was relatively mild, believing that she had committed a great sin by enjoying herself in that way. Nothing he could say would comfort her guilt. She simply believed that it wasn't normal. Morgan's sex drive was very high, and she never denied him. But her unfounded guilt was painful to watch. When he proposed, she accepted with the condition that they would not participate in the rough play anymore. Because Bruce loved her, he relented and put those desires to rest. By the time they were old, he had forgotten how much he enjoyed rough play. And he had become a stale, vanilla old man. He had forgotten who he was. But he never regretted any of it. He loved Morgan and would sacrifice anything for her.

But Kilra reminded him. As he regenerated, he became more aware of who he was when he was a younger man-who he really was. And he remembered those times he acted as Morgan's dom. And the longer he was with Kilra, the more he remembered those wonderful fucks in his back field-the time before Morgan also gave up on her true self.

WHEN VAREK AND MORGAN got back to the temple, Varek showed her the chamber she would be staying in for the next few weeks. It was modest, but roomy and comfortable. Morgan was sitting on the bed doing the breathing exercises that Varek suggested. She was still exhausted from the wedding that just took place not much more than a day ago. But she was restless, and Varek said she should try to relax because the evening wasn't yet done.

As Morgan was in her room contemplating the studies she would be undertaking, there was a knock on the door, but before she could answer, Bruce walked in.

'Bruce! Its...'

But Bruce held a finger to his mouth and strode over to his wife. He whispered:

'*Shh. Be quiet, Morgan. I have business with you, and I don't want Varek interfering.*'

'Bruce, what is this about?'

Bruce then embraced Morgan tightly and held his hand over her mouth. She began to struggle to get free, but he held fast. Then he lowered his mouth to her ear and began speaking to her in breathless whispers. She could feel heat coming off him, and a familiar hardness growing more and more insistent.

'*Listen carefully, Morgan. And if you cooperate, I will remove my hand from your mouth.*'

Morgan, not having any of this, began to struggle even more, causing Bruce to tighten his grip and press himself more firmly against his wife.

'*I will not ask again. You have been mine for over 50 years. And I have loved you. I have allowed you to come to this god-forsaken world for some dream you have of making a difference. And you have allowed these alien men to take you in all kinds of ways.*'

Bruce saw tears streaming from Morgan's eyes, but they also flashed with anger. But Bruce was relentless. And aroused.

'*But I'm going to make you remember who I was to you before we were married, before our mistakes, before we grew old. I'm going to make you remember who we were together. Stop struggling Morgan, this is going to happen.*'

Morgan's breathing slowed. She knew he was right. But she was not going to give in. She kept struggling.

Bruce then lifted her up and laid her on the bed. He got on top of her and rested most of his body weight on her. He loved the flash of anger in her eyes. She was going to enjoy this, and so was he. He bent to her ear and continued to whisper in hot, quick breaths.

'*Do you remember two weeks before our wedding? We went dancing and you began grinding against me, teasing me mercilessly. You loved to tease me back then. Then when we got home you teased me more and then said you were tired and going to sleep. Remember? Nod your head if you do, sweetheart.*'

Morgan nodded her head. She did indeed remember. She wanted to be in control, and she loved seeing him miserable with desire.

'I thought you might. On our wedding night we made love. But that particular night, I fucked you hard. I made you remember who you were marrying. After, I thought I was too rough, But I wasn't, was I?'

Morgan wasn't going to give an inch. She just looked at him. But she knew it was true. While they were dating, they played it rough sometimes. She loved it. But she was conflicted because of her faith. She told Bruce after they were married, they needed to stop.

'Do you know how I knew you liked it? Your pussy was never more wet than that night. Ever again. But you were angry. Just like you are now. And you wanted your lust quenched as soon as you regained your youth, didn't you? So you allowed yourself to be seduced by these creatures. The fact that you could save Earth, well. That was just a bonus.'

Bruce took his hand off of Morgan's mouth. She started to struggle again.

'Stop it. You know what comes next. When I am done with you, you will remember who I am to you. You see, even when I am fucking those aliens, I close my eyes and think of you. They know it, and they don't care. Because that is who they are. What I want, and what I will have after today, is that no matter how much they make you cum, You will remember me and yearn for me to fuck you like I did before we were married.'

'Bruce.'

'What? What can you say? I know you love me. But before I release you to these creatures again, you will know I love you. Are you ready? Let's see.'

Bruce took his left hand and lifted her robe up to her waist. He was pleased she wore no undergarments.

'Ah. This makes it easy. Let's see what you have for me. Stop struggling. I am going to give you every inch, and you are going to love it. Open your legs now. Or I will do it for you. Don't worry. I won't make it too easy. I want you to feel how deep I can go.'

Morgan tried to clamp her legs together, but she had already begun to be aroused, and wetness was moistening her inner thighs. He easily slid one of his fingers in. He looked at her and smiled.

'Oh yes. You are willing, but not ready. See. I've also learned some things while I have been with these creatures.

Morgan sat up and slapped Bruce hard against his face. He quickly straddled her, putting his hand against her mouth again.

'*If you continue to struggle, I won't care if Varek comes in. All he will see is me fucking my wife. But you don't want him to see us, do you? It's different when it's us, isn't it? You don't want them to see too much of your human side.*'

Bruce got up from the bed and unzipped his pants. He didn't have any undergarments on either. No wonder. His dick was huge and hard as a rock. He was pleased that she looked afraid. He finished taking off his pants.

Morgan got up and tried to brush past him. He grabbed her at the waist just as she was about to slip away. He held her to him while he began to take his hand and rub her moist lips, then he took his middle finger and tickled her clit rings.

'*Oh sweetheart, you're getting so wet. Why are you trying to run? We're not done. Sit on the edge of the bed and open up. I've been thirsty for your pussy and I'm gonna get my fill.*'

Morgan didn't know whether to be angry or excited. She was afraid she was about to give in. She had not seen Bruce like this since before their marriage. He was fierce and the fact that he kept whispering sent shivers down her spine. She slid backwards on the bed and tried to clamp her legs together, but Bruce grabbed her by the waist and slid her back to the edge. He forced her legs open.

'Bruce, please. What's gotten into you? You know I love you!'

'*Yes. I know. And I love you. But you need to remember that other part of me. The part that would kill for you. You need to remember how thoroughly I can fuck you. And I need to know if I can give you more than you can get from your other so-called husbands. Now keep your legs open sweetheart. I've got work to do.*'

Morgan did as she was told, and Bruce got to work. He slowly started licking her labia and clit until she started to groan, and when she was about to cum, he stopped and stood up to look at her. She had a film of sweat on her face, and she didn't look as angry as before, but he knew she would try to get away as soon as she got the chance.

'*Slide up on the bed, Morgan. Do as I say now.*'

Morgan, still planning her escape, did as she was told. She told herself that when she got the opportunity, she would get away. She didn't know if she liked Bruce like this. He was starting to sound like the predator he was when they were dating. Bruce lay on his side next to her, straddling one of his legs over hers. This gave her full view of his hard dick, stiff with blood and lethal. She wanted that dick. But she refused to let him know that.

He then began fingering her in earnest now, and it was getting difficult for her to concentrate. He put his mouth next to her ear.

'Let go, Morgan. Just let go. I love you. I want you desperately. Look what you've done to me. I'm so hard. When I start to fuck you, to really fuck you, you're gonna feel every single inch and I will take my time. You're getting so wet. I've got three fingers in. There, that's it, sweetheart. Let go now.'

Morgan gave up trying to resist. His fingers felt so good in her pussy. She was starting to feel that bubble building up again. She didn't care anymore as long as she could keep feeling this good. She started grinding against Bruce's fingers.

'Yes. That's it. I think you're ready. You're about to cum. But I won't let you. Not yet. Time for my dick to have some fun, don't you think?'

Morgan opened her legs. She was meek as Mary's little lamb.

Bruce rolled over on top of her and finally kissed her deeply. His warm tongue found hers and just like always, she felt she would have an orgasm from just his kiss. Then he raised up and rubbed the head of his dick against her pussy until he finally just stuck the head in, teasing her. He could feel her throbbing against him, and he thought he would give in himself, but he wanted to see how much she wanted him. Finally, Morgan started to whisper.

'Please Bruce, please?'

Bruce kept teasing her with his dick.

'Please what? You want me to call Jyn? Elrek? Vek?'

'No Bruce. No. I want you to fuck me. Please Bruce! I can't take this.'

'Oh yes, you will take it.'

Bruce then slowly pushed his dick into his wife. Painfully slowly. When he got all the way in, he just pumped it there. He knew the spot he needed to hit. And he hit it. Morgan was just about to cum when he slowly pulled back out.

'Damn you Bruce.'

'Hmm. It's finally time.'

Bruce then shoved himself back into his wife and fiercely thrusted-thoroughly fucking her until she started to moan. Her pussy felt so warm. So tight and wet. Then to be certain, he pulled out and went to work with his mouth again, and this time when she was about to cum, he raised up from her pussy and shoved his dick back in slowly and pumped her until they both came together.

When he pulled out, he pulled the result out with him, his and her mutual orgasms, thoroughly wetting the sheets. He sat on the side of the bed and looked at the love of his life. He had no more need to whisper.

'Do you understand now? I can give you what you need. And I will. You don't need to be ashamed of your desire anymore, Morgan. I certainly won't be ashamed of mine.'

Morgan didn't say anything. She was throbbing still, thoroughly satisfied. She knew that she still wanted him. And she knew he had to leave. She also knew that she loved him more in this moment than she ever had. Because he showed her his fangs, she could show him hers.

'I love you Bruce. And when I see you again, I won't resist.'

Bruce smiled, then he said:

'Where's the fun in that?'

And after that, they helped each other clean up and kissed good-bye.

CHAPTER EIGHTEEN

MORGAN DIDN'T LEAVE her room until dinner time 2 hours later. Varek was waiting for her with some tea and a light meal. He said:

'How was it with Bruce?'

Morgan stepped to the table and sat slowly without answering. Sitting was difficult. Then Varek said:

'He told me earlier he was coming to see you. I saw what he intended to do in his eyes. I thought it would be a good thing. Necessary for your recovery.'

'My recovery?'

'Yes. By necessity you have spent an inordinate time with our people. And more time than usual in intimate relations. As time goes on, Bruce will serve to be a much needed anchor to Earth. We never expected you to give up your Earth blood, but to recognize the Prymiahn blood that flows inside of you. And because your duties to us will change and become more important, when it gets to be too much, Bruce will be there for you. You must always remember that he is your first -Shaed. Your husband-protector.'

Varek started to chuckle.

'What is so funny, Varek?'

'You are angry.'

'Yes, I'm angry. Why is that funny?'

'Because you are angry with him for giving you pleasure. Not the pleasure you expected, but the pleasure of being surprised about a part of him you forgot. And angry because you must wait some time before you see him again.'

Varek then smiled and shook his head.

'Now what Varek?'

'All three of your husbands are hungry for you. And each of them will take their fill at your altar. I hope you are ready.'

'Varek, you are not as funny as you think you are.'

'And you are not in control as much as you think you are.'

'CALM YOUR MIND, MORGAN. Please relax and drink the tea while we go over your training.'

'Thank you, Varek. Tea would be nice.'

As Morgan drank the tea, she found it calming to her mind. Her thoughts drifted away from her husbands. She began to feel more focused.

'Ah. I see the tea is helping. Good. You are miserable, aren't you?'

Morgan began to cry with great spasms of tears. She was surprised at the emotions she was releasing, but relieved to be letting the tears flow.

'Varek, I am so sorry. What is happening to me?'

'This is just the beginning of your training. You will become yourself again. You will only see me in this space. I will not touch you. You will sleep alone and bathe alone. I will take my meals with you so we can speak, and you will read and study the sacred scripts that you were unable to see before. And I will not enter your mind. You must tell me how you feel, no matter how uncomfortable. And that, Morgan, will begin your first lesson and it will be the hardest, because some things you have not yet admitted to yourself. But you will. And when you return to your husbands and your duties as the Revered Mother, you will be in control of your passions, and that of your husbands.'

Morgan sat dumfounded. But she felt so much better, just knowing she would have her body and her mind to herself. Varek continued.

'I will start with what *I* must. And you will listen. We knew you when you were a child, Morgan. We had been on your planet for decades before the invasion. We have influenced your media, planted seeds of lust in your people, implanted our alien infrastructure within your own-all to prepare your world for conquest. Your grandmother was raped by one of our scouts long ago. He was killed for his transgression, but you were watched carefully. Your mother almost went mad because of her lust. She had no idea where to fulfill it. And she would never be able to. But you were able to manage, and you found the best part of us within you. Then at puberty, we sent you a dream, but it not only activated your mental abilities, but it also gave you an almost insatiable sexual desire. And we knew then that we were the only ones that would fulfill it. That was your *first* rape, Morgan. And you were so young. What you must realize, is that conquest for us-bondage-always begins with the mind. It is to us a gentler way to ease the suffering of the worlds we colonize. But it is no less cruel. You were no more able to stop us then and without the rebellion, you would not be able to stop us now.'

In her heart, Morgan knew this. But to hear Varek speak to it so plainly. It saddened her and made her angrier. Varek poured her another cup of tea.

'Drink deeply, Morgan. I am not done, and you must hear it all. Then you will rest. The tea will help your focus and keep you from allowing your rage to overtake you. It is tremendous.

'You were always meant to be the Revered Mother. Most of us want to end colonization because it is simply not needed. And it was never meant to be what it has become-an excuse to ravish worlds. You are our last hope for redemption. Your love for us has not faltered even with the suffering you have experienced and are still experiencing. Your love is the only thing keeping you from despising us until your death overtakes you and gives you rest. Jyn was chosen for you but did not expect to fall in love with you. He was ambitious and wanted the mission to seduce you. I found it humorous that he fell so deeply in love with you. Serves him right, he's always been so arrogant. But Elrek-he loved you from the beginning. He saw in you what I did. A rare jewel to be cared for. They both love you deeply. And yes, I desired you too. And the gifts I would have given you would have been many. But Elrek is even more gifted than I. He is just unaware of it. You have already helped him see. But he will see more when you return to him. And Bruce is finally taking his rightful place as your first Alpha. Wouldn't you agree?'

'Yes.'

'And yes, you have always been correct in your thoughts. We raped the earth. We raped you. We trapped your people in bondage without them knowing and gave them the illusion of choice. That is nothing more than rape. But you endured for the love of your world and for ours. Your Prymiahn DNA kept you stronger than most. And yes, I knew when I chose you that your rage would burn. I needed you to hate us and desire us too. That is the perfect balance between Savage and Saint.'

Morgan continued to listen quietly. Nothing Varek said was a surprise. She also knew that this was not the hardest part of her training. She was correct. Varek poured another cup of liquid. But it was not the same tea. This one was bitter, but it opened her mind a bit more.

'Morgan. You must speak your truth to me. You will not like hearing the raw words. But you must hear them coming from your own lips, and I cannot force you. Today is the day you will begin to become more of yourself than you ever had. But first you must see who you truly are. Speak child and be at peace. It is as it should be.'

Morgan, mentally anguished and uncertain, began.

'I have always felt out of place on Earth, and I was always angry. I was full of desire with nowhere to place it, and as I got older, I just felt lost. I wanted to escape. When I was younger, I cried out to the stars, but got no answer. I decided that my faith would save me, and it did. But even then, I was not fulfilled. I kept searching for a deeper meaning than what my life had to offer. I felt the invasion before anyone else did. I know that now, and I was relieved. I knew the night Jyn came to me that I wanted him. I was ashamed at first because I thought of my age. But my desire had not been quenched in so long and I was so hungry. I was hungry for pleasure yes, but hungrier for knowledge. For knowing that something bigger than earth existed and that my life could mean something. I knew I was in bondage, but I didn't care. I was angry that I didn't care. I was angry that I wanted Jyn. But my lust was too great. I knew I wanted to be with him, and I wanted to shed the confines of Earth.'

'But that's not quite all is it?'

'No. When Jyn took me the night of the Vrek-Mal, I enjoyed it. The pain and the pleasure. I was finally able to have my lust quenched. We had fallen in love. But when I connected with his -seye, my lust for knowledge was also quenched. But only for a moment. I was still hungry. Still full of lust. I enjoyed being around Elrek-but in a different way. I loved him more deeply and wanted him more. It didn't help that Jyn was so agreeable. Varek, this is awful. Why must I go through this?'

'Because your Prymiahn blood is dominant. You are losing the person you were as a human and becoming more like us. Your lust for knowledge and your desire to commune with our -seyes is normal for Prymiahn women. You must accept the fact that it will be normal for you for the rest of your life. Your physical discomfort is because you are fighting to keep your humanity. You will only keep enough of it to remember that you must avenge your planet. Not just for earth, but for the people you belong to now. I have one more cup to give you, but not until you tell me what you don't wish to. You will be ashamed at first. But this is part of your healing now. Training for the day is almost done. Tell me.'

'Varek.'

'Tell me child. I will not ask it of you again.'

'I am miserable with desire. All the time. I am hungry with it. Always wet. Always full of need to be filled by my husbands. My Attendant tries to quench me, but now he must simply push me into sleep. I cannot sit comfortably. The only time I feel better is if I get Jyn to force me. And it seems that the more aroused I am, the more my husbands are, and it's a cycle of misery I can't seem to be free of.'

'I see. Your human side is fighting for dominance. Your vagina is not accustomed to this type of activity, so you are miserable. Even with the partial -seae Elrek has created for you out of his love is not enough. Your mind is so much stronger than you know, so it fights from being overtaken by one side or the other. This has created damage to you physically. Your -seae cannot function as it should because your mind is afraid that if you let it, you will lose what's left of Morgan of Earth. Is that so?'

'Yes. I feel if I allow it, I will forget who I am. And then, I will forget Earth and the suffering of my people.'

Varek placed a large chalice on the table and poured something into it. He said:

'You will never forget your origin. Bruce showed you that. And now you see why he is important for your recovery. And you will never forget the people of Earth. But each day your Prymiahn blood fights for dominance and will soon overtake you. You must let it do its work. You will be surprised to find mercy there as well. Your control will be greater, not lesser. But so will your desire for your husbands. Even Bruce. You will need him more as time passes, because his strength will remind you of what you are fighting for. But you belong to Prymiah now. You have been Earth's child long enough. You will drink now and begin your healing. It is fermented Guardian fruit. You will drink all of it, and every morning until your training is over.'

'What will it do?'

'It will heal your wounds. But it will finish creating a -seae within you as well. You can no longer live comfortably without one. It will not be sentient at first, but it will be completely functional otherwise, and even Bruce will be pleased. After you have been trained, Elrek will come to you, and you will go into my private garden. And after he has finished you, your lust will no longer control you, but you will control it.'

'I'm afraid Varek. I don't want to lose myself.'

'On the contrary, Morgan. You will finally find yourself. I am going to leave you to drink the wine. Drink every drop. You will immediately notice your intimate swelling going down and its hunger beginning to leave you. Once you are finished, go take a bath. I have placed all you will need in your chamber. Then rest. You will probably sleep for a couple of days. When you awake there will be food on the table, and we will eat. And after, we will read the holy scripts and I will teach you how to mix the sacred herbs. Because when you awaken, you will be ready to learn. And your vagina will be gone.'

The next morning, Morgan lay in bed completely at peace and not the least bit aroused. Then she thought about what Varek said and reached down to touch herself. She was shocked at how quickly her own touch aroused her. She reached for the mirror Varek placed for her on the side table to see for herself what was there.

She noticed that she had a few extra folds, small and delicate. Very sensitive to the touch. They seemed to have a mind of their own, moving against each other when she felt them. She still had her human labia, and her clitoris was still intact. But when she stuck her finger in, she felt what must be tentacles and just like the folds, they began to swell and throb with the slightest touch. But when she removed her fingers, her arousal lessened, and she felt normal again.

After she finished her bath and dressed, she met Varek in the outer garden, as he instructed her to do last night.

As usual, Varek was waiting with hot tea. She was thankful for it. He said:

'For the next few weeks, based on your progress, you will be Vok-Tor training in the mornings, and the time we spend doing that will depend on my determination of your readiness to move to the next phase. I will be hard on you, and you will hate me for it. But all of it is to keep you safe and able to defend yourself. After, you will bathe in a healing bath, with the ingredients that you will learn to mix yourself. I will help you mix the first few doses. You must be precise in the measurements. These formulations are ancient and if mixed incorrectly can have unwelcome effects.

Of course, I will show you how to mix more dangerous doses, that can be used against an enemy, or placed on a bow-tip to paralyze prey. There is even a protective ointment I will teach you to make that you rub inside of yourself when you are in enemy territory. Prymiahn women are sometimes kidnapped due to their sexual attractiveness, and the main form of torture for those that participate in those atrocities is rape. Our women know this and place the ointment within them before they travel. If a man enters her to rape her, the ointment enters his bloodstream and kills him. Quickly. Most of our galactic neighbors know of this and thankfully leave our women alone.

In the evening you will study the holy scripts. You will see our origin and why things are the way they are. It will continue as such for several weeks. I will know you are ready when you can put the tip of your blade to my neck and draw blood. Then you must fight me off of you because that will enflame my desire and I will not be myself. So you must continue to battle me in your exhausted state until you subdue me, and my passion subsides. You must not under any circumstances relent. If you do, I will ravish you and you not only would have failed your training and have to start over but gained yet another consort.'

'Can we skip that part Varek? I mean, can't you tell I'll be able to fight you when I can draw blood?'

'You may have to fight Prymiahn men. When they fight females, it arouses them. The more powerful the female, the more excited they get. They become stronger when they try to subdue them. That is why our females are so fierce. And why our men know to leave them be. But you are the most desired because of your beauty and rank. One day you will be tested. Of this I am certain.'

'But I have no doubt you will subdue me, Morgan. By the time we get to that point, my audacity will anger you and you will be glad to teach me a lesson.'

Morgan just looked at Varek curiously. He was big himself. And thick with muscles. She found it hard to believe she could ever subdue him.

Varek just smiled. He knew he would push her to her limit. He knew he would try to ravish her because a deep part of him wanted her. But he also knew he will end up bloodied and bruised because she won't allow herself to fail. He was pleased.

'After that, you will be released to take regular training with your family in the dojo. You can rest assured that they are going through their own trials. But before that happens, you must allow Jyn and Elrek to finish you. You will be strong enough by then.'

'Okay, Varek. Let's get on with it. I'm anxious to be done.'

'You will have one more task before you are released to go home.'

'Of course.'

'You will go alone, deep into my garden where Vek will show you his true self.'

'What does that mean?'

'I cannot say.'

'I trust him Varek. He is my Guardian.'

'It is as it should be.'

CHAPTER NINETEEN

TRAINING WAS DIFFICULT. The physical training had Morgan sore for days. But Varek was relentless. Sore or not, she had to fight through the pain. She enjoyed learning about the different herbs to use as aphrodisiacs, and healing poultices, and the various plant oils used for anointing and bathing. She took to those recipes quickly, which pleased Varek, because he was known to be proficient in this. And she also enjoyed reading the holy scripts, but she was quite surprised with how erotic they were. One day she found a small golden box that contained a page with writing she did not recognize. It was not Prymiahn. She took it to Varek and asked him about it.

'Oh yes. That is the only record our people have left of the writing of our hosts. It is curious that you would find it.'

'What does it say Varek?'

'It says, "The serpent has forced its way into my temple and bitten my heart. I am undone."'

Morgan shuddered.

'Tell me, child. Why did that statement make you tremble?'

'It reminded me of the first day I saw Jyn in his true form. When I saw his symbiote. At first I was repulsed. It was so foreign to me, and it just seemed too *alive*. If that makes sense.'

'I think I understand, go on.'

'I could hear it sliding out of his folds. The slick thickness of its fluids filling my ears with dread and something else I didn't want to think about. I pushed that thought from my mind. And the mouth-it just seemed impossible. I didn't want to get near it. But I was drawn to it somehow, and when it made its way inside of me, it felt like it was pushing itself in, crawling in. And I could hear its slippery yearning. At first it hurt. But as it got further in it began to undulate, like a snake, pulsating and finding every part of me, and when it did, I would go further into arousal until I finally came. It felt delicious, and lustful, and insistent. It also felt dark and wicked. So I was frightened I had slipped into a rabbit hole I would never escape from. And I was right, Varek. Because I wanted that feeling again and again. Even now, I yearn for the feeling of my husbands and Guardian inside of me. And I stay open for them constantly. Throbbing and wet. Waiting for them to take me again. So yes. I feel undone.' Varek just listened. He knew she would always need to be filled by her husbands. And they would need to be received by her. It was life to them both-the exchange of knowledge is never quenched. As she was speaking, he felt his own symbiote swelling with anticipation. It was unfortunate he would never dwell in her garden himself. He just looked at her gently and smiled. Then finally he said:

'It is as it should be.'

THE DAY SHE DREW BLOOD at Varek's throat was a surprise to them both. She was angered by a dream she had of a time on Earth where she was assaulted. She had forgotten about it, and she woke up angry and in a cold sweat. She was itching to spar and in her aggression bested Varek quickly. And as he warned, it enflamed his passion. He hissed and pinned her down, rubbing himself against her and trying to take off her gear. She didn't expect to be aroused herself, and that made her even angrier. So she proceeded to beat him bloody and when it was over, her knee was on his chest and her blade was at his throat again. When she realized what she had done, she started to laugh because she remembered what Varek had told her.

'Morgan, my child. You have passed. Jyn will finish you tonight.'

Morgan was glad. She was downright horny. She hadn't been touched by any of her husbands for three months. But it was kind of nice. This was the first time her desire was her own since all of this began. She reveled in it. She was looking forward to seeing Jyn, but she knew she would soon be seeing Bruce, and that thought alone made her wet. Later that evening, Varek gave her instructions.

'Go into my outer garden alone. Jyn will be there with Vek. They know what they must do. Slowly remove your garments and lay on the ground. Entice Jyn. You know how. He is already anxious to have you again. But he must pleasure you completely. You must not assist him in any way. It is his job to finish you. If you are at peace and sated when he is done, he has completed his task. If not, Vek will finish you and kill him. These moments will be the only time I will be in your mind. I will know when the task has been completed. You will return here to be refreshed and Vek will discuss matters with Jyn.

'What will he discuss?'

'Where Jyn can improve his technique, of course.'

'You're not serious.'

'I am. After this is over and you return home, you will be glad you know how to make the healing ointments. Your husbands will be competing to bring you ultimate pleasure.'

VAREK KNEW THE MOMENT it happened, of course. And he was relieved that his brother still lived. When Morgan arrived, she was walking carefully. She looked tired, but lovely. And satisfied. After she had bathed, Varek asked her to the table. She thought about all of the wonderful conversations that were had at this very table. She was going to be sad to leave.

'How was it with Jyn, child?'

'Different. I felt like my emotions were all over the place, but he met me at each one. But he wasn't the same. Usually, he is more forceful. This time he tortured me with desire first. It reminded me of Elrek.'

Varek listened to all that Morgan had to say and was amazed. Being from Earth and having no knowledge of the Prymiahn faith beyond the drops of its blood inside of her, she was beginning to understand her power. When Vek was done with her, she would understand more.

Just then his brother Jyn walked in. Varek noticed that he also, walked haltingly and slowly. He saw the shy smiles that Morgan and Jyn shared. And something else was on Jyn's face that Varek had not seen in a lifetime. Humility.

'Well, then my brother. Come sit and share tea with your wife.'

Jyn sat across from Morgan, and Varek was pleased to see that his face was flushed, and his breathing began to quicken just being in her presence. Morgan, however, was as content as a cat that has just feasted on its prey. She excused herself to take a nap, and Varek smiled and thought how cat-like that was as well. After all, once sated, there is nothing left to do but rest. But as she left, she kissed Jyn on the neck, which caused him to tremble slightly.

Once she was gone, Varek just looked curiously at his brother. Jyn said:

'Well, Varek. Get on with it.'

'Was it well with you, brother? You look completely undone.'

'It was as it should be.'

'Oh no. You can do better than that. I am your brother after all.'

Jyn hissed. Then he said:

'First, I'll show you.'

Jyn then opened his folds for Varek, as his -seye would not retreat from them voluntarily. It was glowing blood red. It had retreated far into Jyn.

'Is it painful?'

Jyn smiled.

'Oh yes, Varek. Still it slowly throbs and burns. But...'

'You are sated.'

'Yes. I cannot give any more of myself to any other.'

'It is as it should be. Although, I think you have experienced something holy. Stay here a few days. Your -seye will need to recover. When you return to Kiisma, you will be quite swollen and ready to bow at her altar as well.'

A few days later, after Jyn left the temple, Morgan was in the library reading again.

'Morgan, take a break from your studies. Elrek will see you this evening.'

Morgan knew this was coming, and she looked forward to seeing Elrek. She followed the same procedure as with Jyn, but it after it was over, she was shocked.

WHEN MORGAN GOT BACK from her encounter with Elrek, she could barely move. She told Varek she would need some time. When she was done bathing, she went to Varek to tell him how things were, which was required of her.

'Morgan, tell me how it was with Elrek.'

'He ravished me. He was unlike himself. Just like Jyn. It wasn't painful, but unexpected. He wouldn't let me up until he satisfied me. And when he was done, well, he stood up and looked at me as if he had conquered me. I was incredulous. And aroused again. So he mounted me again and allowed his -seye to take control.'

When Elrek came in a few moments later, Varek was surprised to see the look of confidence on the face of a friend who had always moved with humility. He strode over to Morgan, lifted her up and took her to her chamber. Varek was amused of course, but he felt for Morgan, who had little time to recover. When Elrek left the room, he sat comfortably with Varek.

'Tell me friend. How was it with you?'

'I was overcome with desire for her. I couldn't get enough. But even then, she was hungrier for me. And each step I took that brought me closer here, I was more and more thirsty for her, and I made up my mind that I would drink from her or die.'

'And your -seye?'

'It is. Restless.'

'You may not have Morgan again. Not yet. You must leave and find Kiisma. Spend your desire on her.'

Elrek left quickly. Varek considered what had happened. They were both finished by Morgan. They were able to let their opposite tendencies express themselves and in that way not only did they finish her, but themselves. He was amazed. But she was not done.

Varek said her final test would take place as she walked into his inner garden alone. It would not be the outer garden where it was safe. The inner garden is wild. She was afraid. She was instructed to wear nothing but the sheer prayer robe that he laid across her bed before she left. She could wear no shoes and her hair had to be loosened from the tight ponytail she wore during Vok-Tor training.

MORGAN SLOWLY WALKED to the deep part of Varek's Garden. She loved everything about Prymiah except for this area. It was wild and untamed. She felt like she was being watched.

She halted when she stopped hearing the animals stirring. The air got heavier, and her own heart started to beat faster. Before she could break into a run, Vek was beside her. She caught her breath.

'Morgan. Don't resist me again. Not after tonight.'

He said it as if it were a command. She did not argue. She stayed quiet and willed her thoughts to calm down.

'Good.'

Vek cupped his hand on her cheek. It was warm and soft, but Morgan felt strength there. He pulled her to him. Close enough for his folds to touch hers, and then he growled softly along her neck. He whispered:

'You feel my folds swell. My symbiote is straining to be set free. He wants to be inside of you, Morgan. I want you to feel my desire.'

Morgan did indeed feel his folds swelling. It reminded her of Bruce, when they would dance, and he would get hard. She loved that feeling. But she was scared of the feeling she was having now. Her breath started to quicken.

'You are afraid. But the fear won't be with you long. I know what you need, and you will have it.'

Vek took his hand and placed it inside of Morgan's robe, gently caressing her breasts, and pausing at her nipples.

'Your lovely breasts are preparing for what awaits them.'

Morgan could feel her arousal building. She didn't want to let it. She wanted to maintain control.

'You cannot control this. I am in love with you. And you will receive all of me. Bruce satisfies the part of you that needs familiarity and stability. Jyn satisfies that aspect of you that craves the primal now and then, and he also satisfies your enjoyment of luxury. And Elrek. Well, Elrek satisfies that part of you that enjoys intimacy without bounds. And you enjoy how powerful he is. But Morgan, I will satisfy all aspects of you. Completely.'

Vek slid one of his fingers inside of her. She groaned, despite herself.

'Your groans will deepen tonight, as will your screams. I need you to see me now'

Vek stood back from Morgan and let his robe drop. It seemed the moons shined on him just then. And Morgan saw them- golden etchings encircling his waist, chest, and thighs. He turned around and when he moved his hair, there they were again from the base of his neck to the top of his glutes. They were absolutely beautiful. Even his hair had golden strands.

'Morgan. I am not just Prymiahn. I am something else. I had to wait until you were ready to see my true being. It pleases me that you think my etchings beautiful.'

Then Vek lay on the warm ground and invited Morgan to join him.

'Let your robe drop, now. And recline here with me.'

When Morgan leaned in closer to Vek, she could feel his desire coming from him in waves. He dug his face in her hair and grasped her buttocks firmly, almost painfully. Then she heard the familiar sound of his symbiotes releasing themselves from their folds. But something she did not expect happened. They intertwined to form one symbiote, huge and lethal, with one large head. She gasped.

'Yes. My symbiote is ready to take you. And so am I.'

Vek began kissing her deeply, using his tongue to find hers. It reminded her so much of Bruce's kisses, but Vek was more insistent. She was arching her back.

But Vek pinned her shoulders with his hands, and began smelling her, breathing his heat on her, then he spread her legs with his knee.

The symbiote's head pushed into her slowly and it hurt, yes it did, it hurt badly, but she loved it, and he hadn't even started to thrust, and she could feel herself wanting to cum, needing to, but Vek controlled that too. And he groaned as he pushed himself into her, and then when he found his mark, he began to thrust. And she finally found her voice, but it came out as a scream.

AS THE COUPLE LAY ON the soaked ground, Vek told her:

'I have given you part of myself, Morgan. It will remain. Look at your thighs.'

Morgan had etchings on her thighs that matched Vek's.

'They are on your back as well. I am your mate, and you are mine.'

Morgan fainted.

SHE HAD BEEN TRAINING for two weeks when Vek came to see Varek. He looked like he had a fever and his eyes looked completely black. She felt him reaching for her and she felt herself responding to him. This surprised her, and before she could dwell on the thought, it was gone. She asked Varek about it.

'Morgan, as your Guardian, Vek is meant to serve you of course, but there is something else, that he has not disclosed.

'What does that mean, Varek?'

'He will reach into the darkest part of your being and allow you to feel everything that dwells there. You may not speak immediately. And after a while you won't be able to anyway. Remember when you absorbed his seed? That act was meant to activate his true connection to you when the time comes. And it will soon. You will not only feel your orgasm, but those of his -seyes. And in turn, you will receive all of his knowledge. And his power. But you will be complete. Be careful with him, Morgan. He will not hold back. And he, like my inner garden, is wild.'

'You are scaring me Varek.'

'Good.'

'I've always felt safe with him.'

'You are. But Vek has something to give to you, and he means for you to receive it. But you don't yet believe that you can be safe within yourself. You are powerful, Morgan. Vek is meant to draw that power out of you. And the more you allow him to do his work, the more of your own power you will feel. And when he has finished you, you will know.'

VEK CARRIED MORGAN back to the temple, and Varek waited until he bathed her and put her to bed. She was sleeping soundly.

'She is well, Varek.'

'Yes. I see you have given her the etchings.'

'Yes. She carries the power of the Ancestors now.'

'And that's not all is it, Vek?'

'No. She is my mate, and with those etchings, I have also marked her as mine.'

'Does she know?'

'She fainted when I told her, I think it was from exhaustion.'

'Vek. She is going to be angry.'

'It is as it should be. I knew she was mine when I was inside of her. She is my mate, Varek. I cannot be without her.'

'She is going to be pissed, and she will take it out on me in training, and then I will take it out on Ren.'

'Well. I see nothing but a benefit.'

'You have yet to know our Revered Mother.'

CHAPTER TWENTY

FINALLY, MORGAN WAS allowed to leave the temple and rejoin her family. She had had enough of training. And she still couldn't wrap her mind around what happened with Vek. Besides, she wanted to spend time with Alex and of course, Bruce. All of them still had to train. But Varek and Dr. Ren were due to visit because he said they had some news. She couldn't imagine what it could be, but Varek wanted everyone there to hear it.

As they were relaxing with their visitors, Varek said quietly:

'Ren and I will be married soon.' Morgan was delighted. She said:

'That's wonderful! I didn't know you were a couple! Ren said:

'We kept it hidden Morgan. I wasn't able to have children, but Varek and I had pledged to each other at his revelation. Women that are unable to receive seed cannot marry. We are rare, but it happens. But Varek and I have been in love for centuries. So we found ways to have each other.'

'So, how is it that you will be married?'

Varek said:

'On the night of your consummation, I was filled with so much arousal it made me feel wild and untamed. After I gave you to Vek for healing, I decided to go into the deep part of my garden to pray and be with my ancestors. But I found Ren there. She looked like I felt. At our climax, she received my seed. I gave her a son.'

'How is that possible?'

'It was you, Morgan. All but one of the female guests that attended your consummation are pregnant, and the one that isn't was pregnant already.' Alex said:

'Damn, mom. What has this planet done to you? You need to get back to earth and start a fertility clinic!'

Bruce and Lindsey laughed. Just like Alex to say something completely inappropriate.

Dr. Ren said:

'Well, Alex. You're not far from the truth. Your mother has extremely strong pheromones. And your mother, intended or not, gives of them freely.

When anyone is near her, they have a desire to mate. Your dad can't wait until he can have her this evening. Look at him. Varek will take me as soon as we get home. And you will pounce on Lindsey the first chance you get.'

'What the... wait. Wow. Dad, you're looking at mom like she's a perfectly cooked piece of steak. And yeah. I feel like I'm gonna wear you out Lindsey. I'm sorry.'

Lindsey just giggled. She was looking forward to it. Dr. Ren continued:

'And it's not temporary. Something within her creates not only arousal, but fertility. People are starting to notice. Anyway, we want you all to attend our wedding. That's why we are here.' Morgan said:

'Of course we will. It would be an honor!'

'Oh no, Morgan. The honor will ours.'

'BRUCE, CAN I STEAL Morgan away for just a moment?'

'Sure Ren. That'll give me time to recover!' Bruce acted like he was kidding, but he wasn't.

When Ren took Morgan out to their garden, she had a concerned look on her face. She said:

'Morgan, how are you doing really? You have been through so much in the past two years. I am amazed that you are still sane.'

'Some days I don't feel like I am. But when I was on Earth, I practiced my faith daily. And even though nothing that I am experiencing here follows any of the precepts of it, just having the understanding that nothing happens in my life that is not already known by my god gives me peace. The closest thing that comes to that is your phrase *'It is as it should be.'* That means more to me than anything I have read in your own holy script because it brings to mind the peace I have in my heart that nothing that is happening to me was not already known.'

'I see. But how do you cope with the multiple marriages and the intimacy that requires? It must be difficult. I see other Terrans mentally crash going through a fraction of what you have.'

'I think it's my age. On Earth, I am still considered elderly. I would probably be close to death by now if I were still there. The thing is, it is the knowledge that I have an opportunity to engage on another level that makes me thankful and also, opens my mind to other possibilities. To me, my Savage heart is Prymiahn, but my Saintly one is Terran. I have been made to employ balance. I still pray and ask for forgiveness for so many things. But I have peace.'

'You don't deny your god while practicing our traditions. I find that fascinating.'

'Why are we speaking of this, Ren? You have never been curious about my faith before.'

'Well. How was it when you were with Vek? He is taken aback by you. His face has a glow I have never seen before. It frightens me a bit.'

'Being with Vek was intense. I expected that because Varek warned me. I thought it was just how it was supposed to be. But nothing frightens *you*. So now I'm concerned.'

'And your etchings? Where are they?'

'Around my waist like a belt, then flowing into my upper thighs. Bruce said I have one that starts at the base of my hairline at the back that flows down the center of my back and ends above my glutes. I didn't know it was there, but when I looked at it in the mirror, it took my breath away. It was absolutely beautiful.'

'I see. Have you touched them yet?'

'No. I've been afraid to.'

'Why?'

'I don't know. Well. That's not it. I have my suspicions. I think I heard Vek say something about me being his mate. But I think I misheard him.'

'Oh, Morgan. You didn't. You are actually his mate, and he is yours.'

'I can't speak about this right now. I simply can't.'

'I understand, but it will need to be discussed. Do you know about the Ancestors?'

'Yes. Varek has been teaching me about them. I've encountered them once. I'm due to go back before the Vok-tor tourney.'

'How was that experience?'

'Terrifying.'

'Well, there is a being beneath the realm of the Ancestors. It was here thousands of years before them, and it flows like a river beneath all of Prymiah. It is the soul of the planet. It's mind. It is sentient, very powerful, and very dangerous. The Ancestors draw their power from it. It has no name but

Prymiah. And when we speak of our world as goddess, that being is who we refer to. Only a few people have encountered it.'

'Vek is one.'

'Yes. After training with Varek, hundreds of years ago, he was told to go see the Ancestors for his second test. He was drawn beneath their realm and engulfed by the goddess. He was gone for hours. We thought he was lost. When he returned, he was etched with golden markings. He was also changed. Part of Vek is not from the Ancestors. Part of him is the Prymiahn planet goddess. As he was rising back to the surface, another male symbiote bonded with him because the power of the goddess was too much for his own to bear alone. He said it was quite painful at first. He didn't know they would fuse before he took you. He came to see me after.'

'Is he okay?'

'Yes. But. He is more sentient. More powerful. He was the chief Guardian already, having had that experience years ago. And he commands his most gifted ones to have it as well. If they are worthy, they are blessed as he was. If not, the goddess absorbs them, and they never return. But none have had the fusion.'

'I don't like where this is going.'

'That's why I asked you how you are. You have changed us in so many ways. And now none of us know what is to happen next. Everything that is happening now was not expected.'

'Why did you ask me about Vek in particular?'

'There is an element to Vek, and all of the Guardians that we are not privy to. As Guardians, they carry certain ancient knowledge that makes them powerful. We rarely question them or their purpose. And they have kept us from destruction on more than one occasion. But they are intense and assert themselves without fear of any rebellion. Vek wants to take you to the goddess. He knew you would be etched when he was with you.'

'I don't want to do that.'

'Why not?'

'I feel my faith would be tested. And when I have expressed my choice, I will be absorbed.'

'Don't make that assumption. At any rate, you will have no choice.'

'Excuse me?'

'In Vek's mind, and in his loins, you are his. As much as his own wife. More so.'

'Oh no. Nope. Not again. No more husbands. I mean it.'

'No. Not your husband. Something more. His true mate. You both are connected now. It's a relationship outside of what we understand. But when he needs you, or desires you, he will not ask for permission.'

'I'm gonna have a problem with that.'

'You won't. Guardians are the ones that train us to push people to our will. You remember how at the beginning being with him was like being in a dream? That is why Varek is training you like he is. You must be strong. Mentally and physically. Besides, you enjoy your time with him, even though it frightens you a bit.'

'Not just a bit. He's sketchy.'

'That Terran term describes him perfectly. He will not interfere with your relationships unless he must. He assured me of that. He is still your Guardian, and you are still the Revered Mother. You outrank him, no matter how powerful he is. If he oversteps, you will let him know it, and he will relent. It will anger him, and he will become even more aroused, but he will obey your wishes. Now. Pull up your robes. I want to show you something I suspect about your etchings.'

Morgan did as she was told, pulling them up to her thighs.

'Okay Morgan. Now very carefully, and for just a quick moment, I want you to begin to caress a part of them. And tell me what happens.'

Morgan did so, and her shoulders immediately slumped.

'Not this again, Ren. What just happened?'

'Your desire for Vek quickened. If you had kept it up, he would be here to take care of you. He is never, ever far from you. And he will feel every single time you are with your husbands. And if they don't satisfy you, he will.'

'What if my husbands touch the etchings?'

'Nothing will happen. Those belong to you and Vek alone. Are you okay? You look faint.'

'I'm going to have some wine now and forget every single thing you just told me. And then I'm going to take the next transport to Earth with Bruce. I'm going to grow old like I was supposed to, play with Mandy until she gets her first boyfriend, and die peacefully in my sleep.'

Ren laughed, but Morgan just shook her head.

'Dr. Ren. This is a beautiful place. I know that part of me belongs here. I accept that. But you are pushing me to a limit that I can't come back from.'

'We know, Morgan. We know.'

AFTER DR. REN AND VAREK left, and everyone was tucked in bed, Morgan snuggled up to Bruce and started to cry. It startled him.

'What's wrong sweetheart? What did Ren tell you?'

'It's about Vek.'

'I see. I expected this.'

'How could you?'

'Well. Elrek trains me, and we speak of things concerning to us as your husbands. He told me about Vek, who he is, and how powerful. I know he will push you to your limits. But you can rest assured, I will not leave your side. No matter what. And he told me the possibility of him marking you as his mate. That's interesting.'

'I want to go back home, Bruce.'

'No you don't. Not really. You are tired. A little disgusted. Scared. A lot of things. But Morgan I know you. And you are part of this world in blood and fate.'

'I'm tired, Bruce.'

'Yes. But just for a moment. We are going to see our other spouse's soon. Aren't you looking forward to that?'

'Yes. But I feel so much more normal when I am with you. You just want me to be *Morgan*. Not the Revered Mother.'

'I know. And I can just be Bruce. And now that we spend more time together with our Terran family, you have a safe place.'

'Bruce, please hold me. Don't let me go. Let me go to sleep believing that its just us again, and we are back on Earth.'

'Ok, sweetheart. Just close your eyes. I'm here with you. I always will be.'

CHAPTER TWENTY-ONE

YSA WAS LOOKING AT Vek with that look he hated. A look of total frustration.

'What is it Ysa? You have that look again.'

'Please tell me you didn't scare our Revered Mother.'

'I can't say that. You know how it is. How it must be. She will have a bit of trouble sitting down for a time.'

Ysa shook her head and said:

'You will give her your seed for a child?'

'No. That honor belongs to Elrek. I will be giving the child seed to *you*, my wife.'

'Vek. You will kill me. I don't think I can take that power from you and live.'

'Ysa. You are my wife and have endured my passion for centuries. You deserve to receive my seed.'

'She has your etchings, does she not?'

'Yes.'

'Then she is your mate, and you are hers. That is a blessing to our house.'

'But she will continue to resist me. It's not the same as it was when she believed me to be a normal Guardian. Now that she knows who I really am-*what* I am-she will be hesitant. And I am not permitted to influence her mind.'

'She won't resist you. *I* have never been able to. Let me see. I need to know what is coming for me.'

Vek opened his cloak to reveal his folds. His new symbiote emerged hissing-thick and lethal. And hard.

'Vek. You really are going to kill me. And the more you desire her, the more healing baths I will need.'

'And yet you still you desire me. Do you not? Even now?'

'More so. Maybe I need to speak with her. Assure her that you are still the same to her.'

'Not yet. I want her to decide on her own. But I will not wait forever, Ysa. And I am not the same. Let me show you. But you will also have some trouble sitting afterward.'

'Ah, my husband. I have plenty of oils for my bath.'

THE NEXT MORNING, BRUCE and Morgan walked casually over to their other residence. They enjoyed the walk. It was quiet, and since they were on the royal compound, safe. There were garden areas scattered throughout and they could speak freely.

'Bruce. Do you find that the closer we get, the more we want to see them?'

'Yes. I've given up trying to figure it out. But I'm glad we've arranged to alternate weeks with them and Alex's family. It feels better. And I enjoy you. I enjoy being with you. And loving you. It reminds me of when we were younger. Except all of the ways we desired each other and couldn't or wouldn't express it we can do now. Morgan?'

'Yes?'

'See that bench over there just behind the tree?'

'Yes.'

Bruce led Morgan to the small bench. He pulled her to him and began to kiss her deeply. He knew what would get her motor running. He always did. He lifted up her dress and found he made his mark. She was already wet. He unzipped his pants and sat down on the bench. Morgan was glad to straddle him, lowering herself on his dick, and moving up and down deliciously slowly until they both came.

'Ah Morgan. That hungry pussy of yours. You better save some for your other husbands.'

'You know how I am, Bruce. I always make sure *you* get served first.'

AS SOON AS SHE AND Bruce walked through the threshold, Idra greeted them warmly. Almost giddy with excitement, she embraced Bruce and quickly led him off. Bruce gave Morgan a quick wink and knowing smile. Morgan smiled back, knowing that after he was done, Idra would need more than a healing bath.

For a moment, Morgan listened to the giggles and whispers of the couple and just took in a breath. She loved being with her human family more than anything. But this felt like home too. The familiar smells of pheromones and intimacy, Prymiahn food, and yes, even the atmosphere of the planet with its soft pulsating heartbeat. But before she could relax in that moment completely, she felt both of her husbands reach for her mind. As she turned, she saw them both. They were magnificent.

'Jyn, Elrek. My loved ones.'

Morgan didn't realize how much she missed them. How much she still desired them both. After being with Vek, she opened up even more. Not just physically, but it was as if her Prymiahn side was finally free to be itself, reveling in all that it had missed while on Earth. Jyn said:

'Yes, Morgan. We feel that in you too. Let's go to our garden.'

Elrek took her by the waist, and they followed Jyn into a large and private garden. Morgan allowed herself to get lost in the scents of the flowers, the feel of the ground against her bare feet, and the desire she could feel pulsating from her husbands. They stopped after reaching a clearing surrounded by flowering trees that just barely served as canopies for the sun, allowing flashes of light and warmth to tease them with the breeze. Elrek said:

'Morgan, we need to be with you. We can't decide who...' Morgan stopped him and said:

'Don't decide. Let's enjoy each other in this space. We'll have each other. You see my thoughts. I am ready. And I see yours that tell me you are too.'

Jyn and Elrek slowly disrobed. And then, they removed Morgan's garments. As they did they moved their noses and mouths along her naked body, enjoying her scent. Morgan lay down on the warm ground and invited them to join her. There was no sign of the symbiotes. They all wanted to take their time. Morgan allowed the desire of her senses to dominate, gently caressing every inch of her husbands, with her hands, face, and mouth, finding areas of tenderness that none of them knew they had. She took special care with their moistening and swelling folds, focusing on the distinct difference in feel and taste. She noticed how Jyn reacted to his arousal by arching his back and raising his hips, while

Elrek moaned and softly hissed. She enjoyed licking their folds to orgasm and how the men held each other's hands tightly in ecstatic misery until they came.

She enjoyed how they each found every inch of her with their fingers and mouths, causing her to swell inside and out and how her nipples hardened when they licked them with their rough tongues. She enjoyed how they took turns between her legs, and how each orgasm felt different-Jyn made her spasm and raise her hips, while Elrek's seemed to cause wet heat to drip from the deepest part of her.

It was only then that the symbiotes made their appearance. Thick, stiff, and slick with seed. They needed her too. She lay on her side, and Elrek embraced her front while Jyn snuggled at her back. She could feel their hunger to be close to her, and she allowed it, enjoying the feeling of safety and desire.

The symbiotes slid inside of her at their places. She was filled with them. Elrek and Jyn stayed still while the symbiotes filled her vagina and anus completely and began to throb and move within. She thought she would never feel this good again. She contracted her muscles to draw the symbiotes even further in and enjoyed hearing both of her husbands groan with arousal. They both called her name as the symbiotes took their time pleasuring her. The spoused rubbed their bodies against her and allowed their lusts to take control, staying there for hours while they bathed in the wetness of countless orgasms. Then they slept.

When they awakened, they all sat up and looked at each other. They stayed quiet for a moment. Then they got up and Elrek and Jyn helped Morgan into her robes and they themselves dressed. There was no need for speaking. They were in each other's minds already, declaring love and wonder to each other. None of them had ever had a shared experience like that. It left them breathless.

Later that week, when Bruce and Morgan were about to leave, all of the spouses sat down for a relaxing dinner.

Kiisma joined them this time, looking radiantly pregnant. Morgan said:

'Kiisma, you look absolutely wonderful. Pregnancy is treating you well.'

'Thank you, Morgan. Shaed-Elrek has given us a daughter. I was away at my parents for the past few days spending time with them while you spent time with our husband. It was a nice break. Elrek has been more than a bit active.'

Morgan smiled. She understood completely. She said:

'So, is this number eight? One more Elrek, and that seat on the council will be yours.'

'I may not have a choice, Morgan. I intend to seed you with a child as well.' Jyn chimed in:

'Yes. He is quite jealous that he has no child with you, yet.' Elrek said:

'I will admit that my -Shaed. I could never keep anything from you anyway.'

'Well. It would seem I have no choice in the matter. But can this wait a couple of months, Elrek? The twins will be weaned soon, and I am enjoying having my body to myself.'

Kiisma, Bruce, and Idra were amused listening to this conversation. They could feel Morgan's flood of emotion. And the desire of Elrek to seed her. Bruce didn't mind. He loved being with his wife when she was pregnant with Alex. She was the most beautiful to him then. He didn't get to be near her when she carried the twins because of the importance of that pregnancy. But he would get to enjoy her thoroughly this time. And he was looking forward to it. She was always more aroused when pregnant. And now that she is enjoying her Prymiahn side, He was sure it would be fulfilling for them both.

Elrek looked at him and nodded knowingly. He also felt his wives to be more beautiful when carrying his seed. Kiisma and Idra asked Morgan if she had been taught the correct herbal concentrations to use when pregnant. Morgan told them those were one of the first things Varek taught her. Idra said:

'Good. Our husbands will enjoy you up until the baby comes. You have not experienced that yet. But you will find the experience...intense.'

Elrek could feel the symbiote moving within him. It would not be long before his seed would not be contained.

WHEN THEY GOT BACK to Alex's, it was lovely to see the kids and hear Lindsey laughing at something silly Alex had said.

'Welcome back, you two! Lindsey said. You look beat!' Bruce said:

'We are. We're gonna go on to bed.' Alex said:

'Again?'

'Shut up Alex. Smartass. We're going to sleep.'

And they did.

SOME OF THE HABITS that Morgan picked up on Earth followed her to Prymiah. And she enjoyed being at Alex's residence. He demanded that no Attendants be present, and Morgan liked that just fine. Vek despised it though, so he insisted on visiting at least every other day to make sure Morgan's needs were met. But today was a good day. The house was quiet. Alex, Lindsey, and the kids were out exploring, and Bruce was in the other room making lunch.

Morgan liked to have the bed made up just like she preferred-sheets tucked tightly, and pillows arranged just so. She and Bruce slept in, so she had time to make the bed up while he made lunch. Then she would take a hot shower and be ready to relax in the garden with him. She was at the end of the bed, folding up the quilt. She didn't hear Bruce sneak in behind her, but she felt his breath on her neck.

Bruce had come in to tell her that lunch was ready, but he found her naked at the end of the bed, standing and folding the quilt like she used to do at home. Except this Morgan was young, with full hips and curly black hair cascading down her back. He had on his robe to go to the kitchen, but as he watched her, he slipped his robe off. He was quite hard by the time he crept up to her.

'Bend over, sweetheart.'

Morgan started. She didn't realize he was in the room.

'Bruce-wha...?'

'Bend over for me.'

Morgan steadied herself with her hands on the edge of the bed and did as she was told. Her breath started to quicken.

'Spread your legs, honey. Yes just like that.'

Bruce gently took his hand and placed it on the front of her bush and flowed his fingers all the way back. He loved hearing her suck in her breath. He knew she wasn't quite there yet, but he would make sure she would be.

'I see why you are so intoxicating to Jyn and Elrek. Your ass is exquisite. Just like you. Get on the bed on your knees. Bend down deep, Morgan. Let's see what else I can find.'

Morgan got on the bed on her knees and bent down, resting on her forearms. Bruce was pleased that she widened her legs a little more. But he had something else in mind. He spread her cheeks apart and saw what he suspected was there. A very small node next to her anus. One meant for arousal during anal sex. He bent down and started lightly licking it with his tongue.

'Bruce.'

'Shh. Let me see what else I can do.'

He started lightly rubbing her asshole with his thumb, being sure to brush the node each time. Just as he suspected, it caused it to open up slightly and it even started to moisten with its own lubricant. Kilra told him that most living beings that excrete have natural lubricants to make it more comfortable when they defecate. That the nodes not only provide pleasure but enhance these lubricants' production to make anal sex more pleasurable. But Bruce also realized that he would need a bit more help. His dick was starting to throb.

'Stay right there, sweetheart. Don't move.'

Bruce was glad he brought lubricant with him. He liked the feel of it, and he knew he would need it. He walked back to his work and rubbed himself generously with it, leaving a great deal of it on his fingers. He then inserted his forefinger slowly inside Morgan's ass. His mouth watered at what was going to happen to her. He put another in and started to thrust.

'How is that sweetheart?'

'It feels good, Bruce. So good, but...'

'You're afraid, aren't you?'

'A little. The symbiotes never get as hard as you.'

Bruce was pleased to hear that. He smiled.

'You're right, honey. I'm getting harder the longer think about fucking your ass. It won't feel the same to you. I've done it to them, and they've done it to you. But you have not had the pleasure of a good, real, human ass-fuck. I wanted to when we were on Earth, but that is the one thing you weren't comfortable with. It might hurt a little. Do you want me to stop?'

'No.'

'Good. Now one more question. Do you want me to start easy and end rough, or start rough and end easy?'

'Let's start easy and see how it goes.'

'That's my girl.'

Bruce slapped his pipe against Morgan's ass so she could feel what was coming. He could feel her begin to tremble a bit. He knew she was nervous. This aroused him even more. He touched her asshole with the head for just a moment before pushing it slowly in. Out and in, feeling the tingling in it. Then he slowly pushed inward until he felt resistance.

'Relax, sweetheart. Relax. You're so tight. I'll have you open by the time we're done.'

Bruce started to rub the node while he slowly continued to push. He felt her heat, she was starting to throb. She started to groan.

'I'm almost all the way in, Morgan. You're doing just fine. I'm going to pull out and give you a rest. But stay on your knees. I'm gonna drink that pussy of yours for a minute.'

Bruce purposefully and slowly pulled his dick out of Morgan's ass. It was opening up nicely. Then he started eating her pussy, sucking it slowly and was surprised that she was so aroused she almost came.

'You're a sneaky one. Hiding your hungry pussy from me. That's okay. When I finish your ass, I'll fix that cunt of yours.'

'Stop teasing me, Bruce.'

'Not a chance.'

Bruce then pushed his dick all the way in her ass.

'Bruce, please...'

But instead of stopping, Bruce started to slowly thrust, being sure to rub the node at the same time. Morgan started to groan and open up a bit. Then she bent further down, allowing him to go deeper. This was their first time, and he wasn't going to rush it.

'How is it now, honey? Still uncomfortable?'

'Not as much.'

'Do you want me to stop?'

'Don't you dare!'

Bruce began to get lost in the feeling of being inside of Morgan this way. He started to thrust faster and before he could think of his next move, he saw the extreme wetness of Morgan's orgasm bursting from her. So he quickly pulled out of her ass and pumped her pussy until he exploded.

As they were resting on the bed, Morgan was amazed at how different anal felt with Bruce. She enjoyed it. But she was sore. She also knew she wanted to do it again. Right before she came, her ass felt tingly and started to throb. It was a weird feeling and she loved it.

'Bruce. Why didn't we do this before? I mean when we were actually younger?'

'For some reason, we didn't feel free enough. Here, nothing is off the table. We don't carry shame.'

They both lay quietly, thinking over their lives, and imagining what they would do to each other next.

CHAPTER TWENTY-TWO

MORGAN REMAINED HESITANT to see Vek. She made herself so busy with Vok-tor training to the point of Varek telling her that she had no choice but to take two weeks off, that the tourney was still a few months away, and he knew she was avoiding the inevitable.

Bruce, Elrek and Alex went on a hunting trip on the other side of the royal compound and would be gone for several weeks. And Jyn was handling state affairs with the council on Morgan's behalf. Kiisma was further along in her pregnancy and just wanted to spend time with Johnathan, David, and Mandy. So she was more than happy to give the other moms a break. Lindsey had been curious about the waterfall spas that were supposed to have rejuvenating properties, so she would be gone for a week herself. Idra told Morgan that this was a time of year where most Prymiahns relax and enjoy their hobbies apart from each other and to get a refreshing time to partake of their own interests away from their spouses. She herself was going on a temple retreat with Ren. She also told her that Ysa would be joining their group. So, Morgan was alone in her thoughts. The door chime startled her.

It was Ysa.

'Ysa? I thought you were joining Idra and Ren on the retreat.'

'I am. But I had some time, and I wanted to speak with you before we left.'

'It's always lovely to see you. I see so little of you with everything else going on, and you were one of the reasons I was able to make it through all of these transitions. Well. You and Vek, of course.'

'Yes. That is why I am here. I need to discuss your hesitancy to see Vek.'

'It's complicated.'

'It shouldn't be. We wouldn't be permitted to speak as we do if it were not for you giving us the authority to do so. You have honored our family for the remaining generations. You have insisted in your actions and example that as Guardians we are to be respected and honored in our callings, above and beyond how we are already. What is your hesitancy in allowing Vek to serve *you*?'

Morgan sat in stillness for a minute. She looked at how beautiful the suns were showering the room with golden light and falling on Ysa like a royal covering. She said:

'I am afraid. It's just that simple. Vek is an enigma to me. He is insistent in my thoughts, and I can't stop yearning for him like he is some kind of nourishment that my body needs. I'm afraid if I give in, I'll lose all control of myself. I felt like that on Earth. I don't want to feel like that again.'

'You won't lose control. You'll gain power. And he is your mate. So of course he will nourish you.'

'I can't see it. Every time I am around him, he overwhelms me with an energy that I can't explain.'

'You can't control it. I can't either. It still overwhelms me after centuries of being with him. It's supposed to.'

'That's not encouraging.'

Ysa smiled. She knew Morgan was struggling. She said:

'Remember when you first met Jyn? He overwhelmed you with your hidden need for holy pain. At first, you thought it was unseemly. But then, when you allowed yourself to accept the gifts he had to offer you, you were free from that guilt. The same with Elrek. He taught you that pain is not the only passion you could feel. That you could allow yourself to accept love and comfort as something you deserve. That it's not just for other people you saw as more worthy. Even Bruce serves you as the one who loves you unconditionally. As flawed as any other being, but one who has seen your worth and would love you through any challenge you face. Is what I'm saying correct?'

'Yes. I can't deny any of that.' Morgan was amazed that Vek told her those same things the night he took her as his mate.

'Vek is not meant to be any of those things to you. He is meant to be the connection between them. The one that centers you and brings out the part of you that enables you to share your gift of unconditional love with everyone that needs you. He is meant to fill you with all of those elements, to replenish you. He is also meant to bring power to you as the Revered Mother. To give you secret knowledge that you need to protect our planet and its people.'

'Ysa. That's a lot. More than what should be required of one person.'

'Not for Vek. He was made for you. He trained for you. His gifts are abundant, and he is anxious to give them to you. And as his wife, I need you to accept him into you, so he can release that power.'

'I don't understand.'

'He was frustrated because he could not release all of himself to me. Not until he had you. If he did, it would kill me. So he held back.'

'Oh no. I'm sorry. I had no idea.'

'He loves me. There is no need for sorrow. But he is devoted to you. I will tell you that the longer he waits when he yearns for you, the more difficult it will be. He will push you to a place you won't expect. And he will be forceful *because* he hungers for you. It will make you angry at first. This is also expected. But he is stronger than your will to hide yourself. You will submit to him again.'

'I don't like that word.'

'I know. But he is the only one you will submit your whole being to. The only one. And you will always be safe with him. He is truly your Guardian. He will kill for you. He would die for you. And so would I. It is our duty as Guardians.'

'I'm still afraid, Ysa.'

'I know. But after you have been with him in the midst of his passion, you will not know fear any longer.'

'What do I do?'

'After I leave, caress the etchings he gave you. Take your time. Close your eyes. Think of him while you are doing it. He will be here when he senses you are ready to receive what he has to give you. He will look fierce, and he won't seem like himself. But he is serious about his duty to you and will fulfill it.'

'How long will this process take?'

'A while. If you are fortunate, just a few days. But he will not rush the process. You will get breaks as he sees fit. But don't be shocked when you see him. He will be dressed for battle as a sign of respect to you. Wear your white prayer robe with nothing underneath it and loosen your hair. You may bathe beforehand for your own comfort, but he will bathe you anyway.'

Tears started to leak from Morgan's eyes.

'Ysa, how will things be after?'

'You will be changed, but you will still be yourself. You will still be wife to your husbands and mother to your children. But you will be the Revered

Mother in body, mind, and spirit and not just in name and you will be comfortable as his mate. As for me, Morgan, I can finally stop taking daily healing baths.'

Ysa smiled warmly at Morgan. Her smile always brought comfort to her.

'I do feel better speaking with you. I am still nervous. But I assume that will subside.'

'It will. But not right away. But you will lean into the process. Now I must go. And Vek knows I am here and is awaiting your call to him.'

MORGAN DECIDED A BATH would be just the thing to relax her frayed nerves. She loved taking them on Earth. But after, she wanted to rinse with the shower. Prymiahns don't typically use those, so she had one installed. Of course it was beautiful. Totally fitted with the walls and floor made of colored glass from the bottom of their ocean and enclosed in a glass so clear that it is impossible to tell if it is actually there except for the handle to get in. All she must do is speak 'Water, warm' and how hard she wants the stream, and it does what its told. She needed one of these on Earth when her arthritis kicked in.

She did not touch the etchings until she was done with her bath. Then she went into the shower. She purposefully wanted it to stream down her back, touching the etchings that were there that she couldn't reach. And while the water did its job, she stroked the ones on her upper thighs slowly and deliberately, just as Ysa suggested. She did not expect the sensation she got when the water hit the ones on her back. She closed her eyes and let the sensation overtake her, recalling the night that Vek finished her, and how she felt. When she opened her eyes she was not surprised to see Vek directly in front of her. Full battle regalia on, allowing the water to continue to splash in his hair and on his face. He looked deadly and he hissed at her, revealing his canines. He took one step and was chest to chest with her. Then he bent down to her ear and whispered:

'You will accept me as your mate.'

At that he lifted her and carried her to her bed, gently laying her on it, and slowly removed his gear.

'Morgan. You know how to speak to my mind without using your mouth, and you can hear me speak to *your* mind. This is how we will communicate. Do you understand?'

'Yes, Vek. I understand.'

'Good. Don't resist me.'

Vek continued to remove his gear slowly. Piece by piece. He watched Morgan as he did so. She was still damp from her shower and was shivering. She was afraid. Vek seemed to catch this thought and smiled. He flashed his canines. Soon he was nude. His symbiote slowly released itself from its folds and Morgan thought it would never stop sliding down his leg. Then he got on top of her and bent his mouth to her ear.

'Vek.'

'Shh. We will take our time.'

Morgan felt the head of Vek's symbiote caressing her insistently. Tapping her -seae at its opening. She could feel herself holding her breath.

'Breathe, Morgan. Breathe.'

'Vek. I'm not ready. Please, Vek.'

Vek hissed in her ear. His breath was hot and sent tremors in her mind. Then the symbiote pushed itself inside of Morgan. Slowly. She was stunned. It did not hurt. But at each movement, each slow centimeter, it created a bubble of arousal and she started to lift up her hips at the delicious feeling of again being filled by Vek.

'Be still, let us do our work inside of you. Relax. No matter what. I want you to feel your arousal build.'

Morgan found this to be harder than she expected. Every time she relaxed; the arousal grew exponentially. She thought she would go mad.

'Morgan. We don't only love each other. We need each other. Just like water, food, and air. We will always need each other. Feel us inside of you. We're hungry too. Open your legs wider so we can grow and lengthen. Feel what happens next.'

'Ooh, Vek! Please! I can't!'

'You can't what? Endure our need for each other? Are you in pain?'

'Yes. No. Not pain. I feel like I'm going to explode. I need to cum, Vek.'

'We won't let you. We're all the way in. We're going to thrust now. You like it when I show you my power. But you have not felt me work with my symbiote. Not like you will now. You will feel both of us.'

Vek began thrusting, but not the frenzied, anxious thrusting that only has a purpose in finishing in orgasm. This thrusting was meant to bring Morgan to the brink of madness. Vek's symbiote began throbbing inside of Morgan, hard throbbing and as it throbbed, it pulled out slowly.

'Vek. What are you doing to me?'

'Showing you the truth of desire. Showing you that orgasm means so much more than what you assume. It is not sexual. It is spiritual. That you have only known a portion of what it means to be fulfilled.'

Vek finally pulled out of Morgan. She was wet with sweat now. Miserable with arousal. She felt swollen with it.

'You are swollen with desire. Your -seae is maturing. It is beautiful. You're wet and glistening. But I am not done with you. We are not done. Keep your legs open wide. Looking at you makes me thirsty.'

'Please, Vek. I'm going to die.'

'Far from it. But you will feel my rough tongue inside of your garden. And you will feel my world between your legs, and I will feel yours in my loins.'

Vek was enjoying this. He was finally able to give Morgan what she needed. And what he needed. He wanted to relish every moment. He had a purpose, yes. But if he was honest with himself, he wanted her all to himself. Just for a little while. And so did his symbiote. So he had to make sure that this moment they had would give her the power she needed. All of it. Because if it did, They would have centuries to feast on each other.

He enjoyed tasting her. Drinking her. She was miserable and swollen. He was taking his time.

'Morgan. Let go. Stop suppressing the discomfort. You have many more hours to wait before your release. Enjoy the misery of your arousal. Close your eyes. Go past the discomfort and let your mind take control.'

He put his hands under her and pushed her even closer to his mouth. He found everything inside of her, and then just when she was about to cum, he stopped.

'Morgan let's rest now. We'll freshen up, and I'll fix us something to eat. Let's take a shower.'

'Damn you, Vek. How am I going to walk? I feel so swollen and I'm just getting over last time.'

Vek laughed.

'I told you that this would take some time. I'm not making love to you. I'm serving your need. And mine. I am fulfilling my duty to you. But make no mistake, my devotion to you goes deeper than any love could. But what I am doing is showing you what true fulfillment is. Come on, we'll shower together. It'll save some time. I'm hungry, and I know you are.'

The cool water felt so good against Morgan's skin. She was glad to be getting clean. She washed Vek's back for him, and he washed hers. Then he turned her to face him and slid his fingers inside of her, slowly manipulating her clit rings. And of course right before she came, he pulled them out. She slapped him hard, and he pulled her to him and kissed her deeply. A lover's kiss. Like Bruce's kiss. And she began to cry because she was so miserable with arousal. She felt his symbiote harden.

'Vek. This is not fair. I feel like I'm going to be sick.'

'Morgan. It's not easy for me either. Look at my symbiote.'

Vek's symbiote was swollen even larger than it was the first time. It was visibly hard. She could see it throbbing. And even though it was lubricated, it had not released its seed. Vek's folds were swollen as well.

'Vek. I am so sorry. Is this worth it? Must this happen?'

'It must. You need this. You do not see it now, but you will. And I need this. To fulfill my duty to you. And my love. When my task is finished, I will make love to you, and you will never be the same.'

Morgan ran to the toilet and vomited profusely. Vek ran to her and held her hair back. Then when she was done, he took a cool cloth and wiped her face. Then he covered her with her robe and led her to the kitchen. They shared a light meal. She was amazed at how hungry she was.

'What happens next?'

'I'll take you back to bed and we start over. Then we'll go into the deep part of Varek's garden.'

Morgan relented her will to Vek. He was simply too persistent, and she was simply too tired. She knew beyond a shadow of a doubt that if she didn't remain and finish her task, she would fail-and that was not an option. Near the end of their session, Vek said:

Morgan. This is not a test. It is a gift. Let me love you. You are still straining against the discomfort of your building passion. This feeling you have is your physical body straining against your spiritual one. Please relax. The sooner you submit, the sooner I will finish you.'

Morgan allowed her mind to rest. She realized that Vek was right. She was still trying to control the situation years after it was too late to do so. She needed to grow to survive. She slowed her breathing and closed her eyes. She allowed the fullness between her legs to do its work, creating a bridge to a reality that she did not know existed.

'Morgan. You are ready. Let's go into the holy place. You must cross the bridge of our Ancestors.'

Vek led Morgan deep into the garden where the nest was already glowing in anticipation of her arrival.

'Vek. Please don't leave me alone.'

'I will not leave the nest. But I cannot go into it with you. You must go alone.'

Morgan had already been through this with Varek. And she knew being afraid was no use. At any rate, it would give her something else to think about besides her discomfort.

But this time, as she lay down amongst the Ancestors, she sunk down underneath them. She was to meet the goddess.

Vek knew she was going to be tested this way. All he could do was wait. She surfaced three hours later. It was morning.

'Vek? What happened? I keep hearing a faint voice in my head.'

'Are you afraid?'

'No. It feels like its always been there. But that's impossible.'

'Morgan, It is time for you to receive my seed.'

Vek led Morgan back home to bathe her before they were intimate. She was very quiet. He suspected he knew why. As he washed her, he felt her arousal build again, but it was muted. Less frantic. She was wearing desire now. Not lust. Like he had always done during her bath, his fingers found their mark. Her response was warm, and she let a sigh escape her mouth. He helped her out of the tub and dried her off.

'Are you ready, Morgan?'

'Yes, Vek. I need you. So much.'

Vek recognized her change. And her desire. He took his time because he knew she was really going to feel him for the first time. All of him.

The goddess had made her -seae sentient. She was now Morgan-seae.

CHAPTER TWENTY-THREE

MORGAN WAS AMAZED AT the sensations she felt. Waves of gentle orgasms followed each powerful thrust of Vek's symbiote. Vek's sighs and moans heard breathlessly in her ear. And Something else. A voice not hers or Vek's. Not heard but felt. A gentle command and the comfort of safety. All of these things Morgan felt as she received Vek's desire.

'Morgan. *The goddess has made your -seae sentient. It communicates with my symbiote, telling him what you desire. And mine communicates with her, telling it what he desires. And your orgasms are now in truth, what the Seae-bereth is. Total fulfillment of desire.'*

And while they were making love, the moment Morgan needed to feel something different-something more aggressive, or more gentle-anything that increased her pleasure-she felt it. Vek swelling and contracting within her, thrusting more aggressively or being still to allow the symbiotes to do their work. And then she just rested her mind and allowed herself to be taken away by her awakening. And then Morgan felt Vek's spines stiffen. But it was not painful. Each spine penetrated each virgin tentacle within her -seae, breaking their seals and thrusting within them. And at once she was no longer there, but traveling to other worlds, galaxies, memories. She was observing the exchange of information between the symbiotes. The true reason for their desire.

She was startled out of the vision by Vek's final thrust. Wonderfully primal and insistent, the spines pulled out of the tentacles at once and Vek released all of himself into her. She finally had her last orgasm. Warm and copious, healing her and preparing her for their next encounter.

'Vek! Have you impregnated me?'

'No Morgan. What I have done is leave a remnant of myself inside of you. When Elrek gives you his seed, that remnant will meld with it and the child will be his in body, but mine in mind and soul. So you will have a child who will be wild, but brilliant. Strong, but merciful. Passionate, but disciplined.'

'Savage and Saint.'

'Yes.'

After they bathed and were preparing their meal, Morgan was pleased at how centered she felt. She was also surprised. Vek said:

'Now you understand the gift I have given you, Morgan. You will now desire. Never lust. Desire is confidence in trust. You know now that you have me. You have your husbands. There is no need to ever doubt that again. Lust is insecurity. Lust is the desire to fuck, to rape. Lust is an attempt to mark territory as yours and yours alone. Desire has no need because it understands that it will always have its needs met when it is time. Lust forces the feeling. Desire lets it happen. Lust looks for its conquest. Desire is conquered by love.'

'It's a beautiful feeling, Vek. When I look at you, I don't lust after you. I don't feel like I did before, conflicted, and guilty. But at the same time I know that we belong to each other and that when we want our desires met, we will be able to come together again when the time is right.'

'Yes. That is why on our world, we don't forbid multiple couplings. There is no need. We understand that the exchange of knowledge comes in many forms. And that the Ancestors created the perfect conduit.'

The rest of the afternoon, Morgan and Vek enjoyed each other's company. The ate lunch in the outer gardens. Walked around the grounds and made love when they pleased. Late into the evening, as they lay together in bed, Vek kissed Morgan softly on her neck.

'It's time for me to return home Morgan. Ysa will be there in the morning, and I am ready to see her. And you will see your husbands soon. The hunting trip will be over in a couple of days.'

'Vek? How long have we been together? It seems like you just got here!'

'We have been together for a little over two weeks. It is as it should be.'

He smiled. Morgan's delight in learning about their ways pleased him greatly.

'But, I am only a moment away, and now you have confidence in this, yes?'

'Yes, Vek.'

And Morgan felt her -seae stir within her, and it gave her comfort.

WHEN YSA ARRIVED HOME, she was pleased to see her husband with nothing on but his prayer robe. His hair was loosened, and he looked absolutely wonderful.

'So, my husband, things with Morgan went well, I see.'

'Yes. So much more than already expected. She was received by the goddess.'

'Is her -seae now sentient?'

'Yes. And she was hungry for knowledge.'

'How many days were you with her?'

'Ysa! So full of questions! But you have always been that way. He smiled. 'I was with her over two weeks. And yes. I released a portion of myself into her, so the child Elrek gives her will be the twin of the one I give *you* tonight.'

'Did you tell her what that means?'

Vek was silent. Ysa gave him that look he didn't like.

'Vek!'

'Well, Ysa. Our Revered Mother...'

'No, Vek! Don't get formal with me! Does she or does she not know what that means?'

'She knows.'

'Does she know exactly? That being a mate carries a stronger bond than any of her spouse's will ever have with her. And not only that-you are her Guardian *and* her mate. So you will know every single time she is with her husbands. All of her joys and sorrows. All of her needs.'

'No Ysa! She can't possibly be ready for what you and I experience. We have had centuries. She has only had a short while. She doesn't yet know the pleasure that comes with that.'

'And the love of devotion. She doesn't know that either. That you love her. Truly love her. That your heart will always desire her, and your loins will always serve her. She doesn't know that?'

'She will grow into that knowledge. I gave her a portion of it. I want to wait until after she has had her husbands.'

'Vek! They will be taken aback by their own desire for her. Especially Bruce. And she will be...'

'The Revered Mother. She will finally be the Revered Mother. Endless in devotion to our worlds and to her husbands.'

'And to you.'

'Yes, Ysa. And to me. But I am her Guardian after all. It is as it should be.'

'She is going to be pissed when she realizes exactly how often she will be in your bed. And of that you may be certain. She will punish you when she realizes that she has gained yet *another* man, devoted to tending her garden.'

'She's not angry. She will control who tends it and when. And that is in her power. She is not a victim. She is the symbol of our faith. And as such, deserves to have her needs met at all times, regardless of what they are.'

'Yet she is still humble and resists her power.'

'Yes.'

'Yes, she is going to be incensed and she will cut you in a tender place. No matter, I will be here with healing ointments when she finds out, my husband.'

'Ysa. Stop this. You just got home, and I desire to give you my seed. I have been waiting to give you a child for centuries. And I want you to feel my need for you. Look at what you have done to my symbiote. Your fussing has made him swell even more. You should be ashamed!'

Ysa laughed. She knew Vek was teasing. Mostly.

'You are right, Vek. I hunger for you, too. But looking at the state of you passion, I am afraid I won't be able to receive what you have to offer.'

'Don't tease me, Ysa. I know you. You delight in having me tend *your* garden, so let me get to work and give you a son.'

CHAPTER TWENTY-FOUR

THE TIME FOR THE VOK-tor tournament arrived quickly. Morgan was more than ready. As Temple Guardian, Vek officiated. And as Vok-tor Master, Elrek would not only be fighting, but judging his students. But when Alex arrived, he had caused a stir. He had shaved his head completely. When Morgan asked him about this, Alex told her that it was a personal matter that he would explain to her later.

Morgan was gifted with the short blade. She had to spar with Jyn, and Elrek, as these were her Prymiahn husbands, and she was expected to best them, but to have a husband best his wife, was a sign that he was dominant. In that case, they would be required to spar again at the next tourney. Jyn was tricky, and almost had her at the end, but she allowed her rage at his impertinence to seize her, and she nicked the side of his throat. It would seem he touched her in a tender spot when they were close. She knew he would do that though, and she was ready. When she sparred with Elrek, she was already flustered because she felt something in him that was wild and untamed. He bested her and when he did, he whispered in her ear that he was looking forward to taking her to the brink. She was glad she was done sparring. He unsettled her in a pleasant way, and she could no longer focus.

Bruce was gifted with the long blade. He easily bested Jyn. His memory of anger helped him with that. But Jyn bested Elrek. He felt a deeper competition with him. A fight for the attention of Morgan. He was finding it more and more difficult to hold on to his time with her, and this would not do.

The next to last expedition was between Alex and Elrek. Alex was gifted in hand to hand combat and swift attack. Since Elrek was his master, Alex felt he had a lot to prove. It ended in a draw, with both of them drawing blood. The observers gasped. It was the longest session they had observed. And it was fun. Both Alex and Elrek were laughing at the end. It seemed that Alex was really trying to kill Elrek. That pleased Elrek immensely.

But Elrek and Vek fought at the last and it was brutal. They were also fighting for Morgan. They both wanted her complete focus, and neither would give it up. Ysa and Morgan watched them with breathless fascination. And both became more and more aroused seeing their husband and Guardian come to blows. They were both getting cut. Ysa said:

'It seems my husband is trying to kill yours.'

'Yes. And I don't understand it at all. I don't like it.'

'No? I am enjoying it quite a bit. Vek will take me roughly tonight. Males are always aggressive after the tournament. You should have your healing oils ready.'

'Oh no. I am due to be seeded by Elrek soon.'

'Morgan, I assure you, it will be this evening. Look at them.'

Both men were now shirtless. There were cuts all over their chests. Everyone was at their feet cheering. Finally Varek, who was the official since Vek was fighting struck the floor with his staff.

'Enough! This session is a draw. Shaed-Elrek and Guardian Vek, you both have proved your worth as Vok-tor masters!'

The whole room shook with the thunder of the shouting audience. Vek and Elrek looked at each other and hissed loudly, enjoying the accolades. Then they smiled at each other and bowed. And immediately after, they both looked at Morgan. They looked hungry. She thought she would be sick.

Ysa said:

'Yes. You will be pregnant in the morning, and I will be sore. Let's meet soon for a mutual bath and breakfast. My Attendant will serve us. I assure you; we will need to speak.'

Morgan's shoulders just slumped. She knew Ysa was right.

LATE THAT EVENING, Elrek had Morgan meet him in one of his favorite spots. A garden that had a well-appointed private area for couples. It was an outdoor gazebo-like fixture with sheer curtains, a bed, a small table for two with refreshments set up by Attendants, and a small chair for the couple to sit. When she got there, he looked surprisingly casual. His hair was in an unbraided ponytail, and he had loose pants on with a linen shirt. His face was glowing in the moonlight, and he looked completely peaceful.

'Morgan. I've missed you.'

'You've only been gone a short time Elrek.'

'Ah. You still don't understand. Come sit next to me.'

Morgan sat next to her husband. He smelled wonderful. Prymiahns always do. But Elrek had a certain scent that she was drawn to. He placed his hand gently on her face, and she loved when he did that, it made her feel precious and beautiful.

'Morgan, it has not escaped me that Bruce and Vek are trying to compete to be your Alpha. And they are allowed as your first -Shaed and Guardian to vie for that position. But you must understand that I will not allow either of them to best me when you are in my bed. You may think of them of course. They are needed by you after all. But it is my intention to satisfy your needs completely. And as I have said, I will bring you to the brink of death if I must.'

'Elrek. You know I love you. What is this, now?'

'I am giving you my seed this evening. But I am also going to remind you who I am to you, just like they have done. I am yours, Morgan. And you are mine. And now you have a sentient symbiote, who must be taught what you truly desire.'

'Elrek you are scaring me a bit.'

'Good. I want you to tremble when I am inside of you. I want you to cry out to me for mercy. I want your pleasure to be so great that you forget about everyone but me inside of you.'

Elrek slowly pulled his shirt off. His chest had a new glistening of sweat. The cuts he got at the tourney were almost completely healed.

'Stand up, Morgan. Drop your robe for me loved one. You will not need it for a while. I am going to enjoy all of you this evening. Of course, I will take my time. And if you need more time, yourself, you will have it.'

'Morgan's hands were trembling as she did what she was told. But she looked at this alien she loved and allowed herself to relax and enjoy the growing arousal she felt.'

'Good. You are not hesitant as you were before. Your 'seae is anticipating me.'

Elrek removed his pants, revealing an already moist and swollen symbiote. Morgan looked at it with unexpected hunger.

'You will have your fill of him, loved one. And I will have my fill of you.'

Elrek lifted Morgan up and gently placed her on the bed. Afterward, he was no longer gentle.

EARLY THE NEXT MORNING Morgan woke to Elrek looking at her lovingly, but with not a little hunger.

'How is it with you, wife?'

'I feel wonderful, Elrek. You know that, though.'

'Yes. I also know that your thoughts were only with me last night. And I'm glad we are outside. Your screams were quite loud.'

'I remember. But don't be coy. I heard you growl. Loudly.'

'Did you like it when I growled?'

'Yes.'

Morgan snuggled up to him and sighed. It warmed Elrek. He loved her most when she needed him.

'Morgan, you have received my seed. The child will be a girl.'

He dug his nose in her hair, she smelled so good. Pregnant women have a smell that intoxicate their husbands. Then he began to stroke her breasts, teasing the hardening nipples. She started to groan softly and snuggled up closer to him.

'Elrek, I want to make you growl again.'

'That would please me.'

'I feel I need you more than ever.'

'You will. It's different when our women are seeded with girls. You will desire me more. It is just the way it is with our people. May I serve your need?'

'Yes, Elrek. But I believe I can make you *roar* this time.'

JYN WAS WAITING AT the door when Elrek and Morgan walked in. He hissed loudly. Elrek hissed back. Morgan just looked at them and shook her head.

'Elrek. Please release my wife to me.'

'If it pleases her to be released, I will.'

'You should have remained her consort. You go too far, now.'

'She is as much mine as she is yours, and now she carries my seed.'

Morgan's face got red with anger. She shouted:

'Enough! Damn it! I thought there was no jealousy between your people!' Jyn sighed and said quietly:

'There's not. I love Elrek like a brother. It is desire that captures us. We can't get enough of you.'

'He's right loved one. It's complicated. Jyn, look at our other wives. They are loving every minute of this.' Idra said:

'Yes we are. The more you two go at it, the more we reap the benefit. Morgan, you have been a wonderful experience in our households, we are blessed!

Morgan looked at them and playfully licked out her tongue.

'I should leave then and let you wives play. I'll go have a relaxing bath, and sleep alone this evening.' Kiisma said:

'Don't you dare! We need rest too!' Then Jyn chimed in:

'Our Revered Mother won't be resting tonight. She intends to go to Bruce soon, and I intend to have her sated by then. Tired or not, Morgan, your legs will open for me.'

'Well, my -Shaed. It may be *yours* that open for me. But we shall see.'

AFTER DINNER, AND AFTER things had calmed down a bit, Jyn and Morgan were sitting alone in their room. Everyone else had disbursed to enjoy each other's company in private.

'Morgan, please consider spending more time with us here. I mean along with Bruce and the twins. We miss you. Idra and Kiisma need you around them. Not just to give them a break from me and Elrek, although that is a part of it. But you are a comfort to be around. Even being without you for a week is too much. You add something to our lives, you really do.'

'We miss you too. I think at first, I had spent so much time with Prymiahns, I lost a part of myself. I was determined to get that back. But I feel more comfortable now. I can go between families a lot easier. Alex enjoys training with Elrek if you can believe it. Lindsey is spending more time with Prymiahn moms and Mandy is settling in nicely. Bruce misses Idra, too. I noticed how they cling to each other when we are preparing to leave.'

'How does that make you feel?'

'He meets my needs when we are together. Seemingly more than ever now that we are here. He is much more assertive now. And he demands what he needs from me, too. But Idra enjoys being his sub. And he enjoys being her dom. So there's that.'

'Yes. I've noticed that when it's time for you two to come over, she gets restless. He arouses her. Just the thought of him. It's not surprising. I think this experience has been good for him, even though at first he hated it.'

'Yes. He told me how he used to get through being with the other wives. I don't think that's the case now.'

'No. Idra says she senses no thoughts of you now. She didn't mind before, but now she feels more connected to him.'

'I think Alex would feel better to have his house to himself and his family. And that is normal, too. Doesn't matter how big the home is. Having your mom in it is a no-no. I'll speak with them when we get back.'

'Morgan. Let's have the Attendants move all of your things here now. They'll have your living area freshened up quickly, although you won't be leaving my bed for a few days.'

'Oh?'

'Yes. Idra has already spoken with Bruce. And Bruce has spoken with Alex. So everything is set in place.'

'All this planning behind my back.'

'Not really. We made certain assumptions. We are empaths, after all.'

'And what is this about me not leaving your bed for a few days?'

'Well. You won't be. We'll take our baths and meals in here. I want to see what it's like with you now that your -seae has matured. And I want to test your limits. Like I did at the beginning. I want to keep you sated.'

'Jyn. You never do anything without reason. What is it really?'

'I love you Morgan. And I desire you. But Vek is very hungry and very powerful. And he will still be your Attendant. And your mate.'

'Have Ysa join him. She will dampen his desire for me since she is now pregnant.'

'Yes. That will do nicely. You really are becoming your Prymiahn self. But you will still stay with me for a few days. I demand it as your -Shaed.'

'I thought I was the one in charge here.'

'You are. But after I am done with you tonight, you will agree. And, well. Bruce is already busy making Idra raw. And Elrek is soaking Kiisma with his seed. So I am anxious to start.'

'Are you men still competing?'

'Of course. It is our goal to keep the Attendants busy preparing healing baths for our wives.'

'I see. And which will you do, husband? Make me raw, or cover me with seed?'

'I am going to do whatever it takes to take your breath away, and of that you may be certain.'

CHAPTER TWENTY-FIVE

THERE WERE WHISPERED conversations between Jyn and Bruce. They were speaking about Kilra's whereabouts. She hadn't been seen in months. Jyn was beside himself. Kilra had been with him on several hundred missions. He trusted her. Now that trust was being called into question. Morgan knew that she would be brought into that conversation soon. And Morgan had something else to be concerned about. She was almost done with her initial training. Then she would be expected to take her place on the council.

But other than that, she was settled into a mostly boring routine, as much as life with Prymiahns can be considered boring. She tried her best to spend her time fairly between Bruce, Jyn, and Elrek, but with the baby coming in a few months, she also tried to get alone time in as much as possible. But now Vek was getting fidgety, and she knew why. She had been avoiding him again. She talked to Jyn about it, and Jyn told her that she was eventually going to need to go to him and let him have his way. As her Guardian, he needs to know of her changing needs, and she may not realize what they are. She told Jyn that he still scares her a bit. One night they were speaking about it more frankly. She said:

'Jyn. I'm just not comfortable with him. I feel like I lose control. And he is so intense. It seems when I am with him, I can't get my bearings. I can't think of anything or anyone but him.'

'Does he hurt you, Morgan?'

'No. Of course not. Quite the opposite.'

'I think I know. You don't want to desire him. You already feel like having three husbands is too much. But he's not meant to be your husband.'

'Then why must I desire him?'

'He's your Guardian and your mate. It can't be helped, Morgan. The longer you wait the more intense he will be. And Bruce, Elrek, and I know why you want to make love in the mornings. You want to be sated when Vek bathes you, so you won't need to be intimate with him. So, for your own good...'

'Don't you dare!'

'You are with me in the morning. And you will be with me tonight. I am not going to touch you Morgan, even though I am swollen for you even now.

But I am going to leave for the dojo early. Remember? Like the first time you were with him? And you are going to let him come to you, and you are going to enjoy him being inside of you with no guilt. And believe me, he will take his time with you.'

'That's not fair, Jyn.'

'Neither is denying yourself the pleasure Vek can give you.'

THE NEXT MORNING, MORGAN tried to entice Jyn to stay in bed.

'Stop it now, Morgan. I feel your heat. And if you enjoy your Guardian this morning, I will satisfy your need this evening. As it is, I am going to stay a bit longer for training, then go to a council meeting with Elrek. And even though you are lovely when you pout, it will not work with me.' Then Jyn gave Morgan a little growl in her ear and bit it lightly, giving Morgan another reason to dread him leaving her.

Not much longer than Morgan was left alone, Vek entered her bedroom. It was very early, and still dark. She was already nude beneath the sheets, so Vek slipped in quickly next to her. He smelled wonderful. She couldn't understand how he disrobed so quickly. She guessed it didn't matter. He growled deeply in her ear as well, and followed that growl down her neck, while allowing his hands to move lightly across her breasts.

'Morgan. Why do you continue to make me wait? You will not continue to keep me from pleasing you. Do you understand?

'Vek...'

'Do you understand me? I know you are frightened by me. You don't want to lose control. I am sorry. That's exactly what I am meant to do, take you away from yourself. Even now, you are beginning to be aroused. I smell your need, your desire. It's intoxicating and I will have all of you. Now do you understand?'

'Yes.'

'I hope so, because if you avoid me again, I will send Ysa to bring you to my bed. She will do it, and you have seen her strength.'

Morgan started to speak, but Vek kissed her deeply, and while kissing her, his fingers found her garden and began to tease it.

'Now Morgan. You aren't as frightened as you may think. Your -seae calls to me. Relax. Stop thinking about what is going to happen to you. Much is going to capture your desire today. Jyn told me to take my time, although I don't need his permission. Nor do I need yours even though you are our Revered Mother.'

'But Jyn is my -Shaed.'

'And I am your mate. And I thought we had an understanding. Stop resisting me.'

'I don't want to fall in love with you!'

'There it is. There is your fear. I assure you, Morgan. It is too late for either of us. Let it happen.'

'Vek. I can't add another to my life.'

'I have been in your life before you knew I existed. The first orgasm you had when you learned to masturbate-I was there.'

Vek removed his hand from between her legs. Morgan's breathing started to quicken. He was in her mind and her body already.

'Yes, Morgan. I am inside of all of you. And I know exactly what you need. Open up to me. I am swelling with seed.'

WHEN JYN FINALLY CAME in that evening, Morgan threw a plate at him and almost hit him in the head. Jyn just laughed.

'It's not funny, Jyn. Vek was here for four hours. I think I have been turned inside out three times.'

'Did you enjoy him? No, don't say. I know you did. You are still aroused. And it's not just because of me. He left you that way on purpose. He wanted you to suffer a little.'

'He's an asshole, Jyn.'

'You don't mean it. You're in love with your Guardian, you are accepting the fact that you are his mate, and you don't want to admit it.'

'Now what do I do?'

'Oh, Morgan. You do nothing. You enjoy him when you desire him. He is not your husbands. Not yet. He is your Guardian. He is on another level from us. And he will always make you feel flustered and out of control. That is his job. Each time you are with him, you will experience another level of pleasure.

And when he comes in to bathe you in the mornings, you will enjoy him like you did before. Ah, yes. You have missed the skill of his fingers.'

'That's not fair, Jyn. And what do you mean *not yet*?'

'Not to worry. Anyway, I find it amusing. I also liked when he fingered you. You stayed wet all day, did you not? When I got home I could slide in quite easily. No matter how swollen I was. And that was before you received your symbiote. Your orgasms were so strong and wet. I'm anxious to see how you feel this evening. And even though you are frustrated with me right now, you are looking forward to receiving me, yes?'

'Yes. Damn you.'

'Don't be that way loved one. Besides, before the end of the week, he will have you again.'

Morgan's shoulders slumped. They seemed to do that a lot lately.

But she was pleased to find that she had plenty of desire left for her husband.

CHAPTER TWENTY-SIX

MORGAN WAS SURPRISED to see Alex, Lindsey, and Mandy come over to her Prymiahn home. When Alex was on Earth, he said he would never cross the threshold of 'those sketchy aliens'. But he looked different. Like he had aged ten years.

'Alex? Is everything ok?

'Yes, Mom.'

Mandy ran past everyone to get to the twins. Jyn was playfully irritated.

'Wow. Not even a hug for this old tomcat.' He winked at Alex.

'Well, Jyn. I really want to see the whole family, and though it makes me almost choke to say it, that includes you, especially. But Dad, Elrek and your other wives, too.'

Jyn and Morgan looked at each other like they had both been struck by lightning.

After they were all seated, Alex began.

'I need to get this all out. So please don't interrupt. Especially you, mom. I love you, but I just need you to listen this time. You asked me why I shaved my head. It's really about you, Jyn. Mom told me about what happened to you on your first colonization.'

Jyn's face darkened.

'It's not what you think, you old tomcat. What struck me, was that you cut off all of your hair to make amends. Your people have the most beautiful thick hair. And I know how Lindsey is when hers gets messed up at the salon.'

This time Lindsey's face had a frustrated look.

'Stop, Lindsey. Let me get this out my way. Anyway, I thought how hard that must have been for you to go around with a bald head when everyone else had their Warriors ponytail. But you did it.'

Tears leaked from Jyn's eyes.

'Oh no, don't get soft on me now. I'll always remember the blade you put at my neck. Anyway the whole point of this is, that I've learned a lot about myself. And being here and going through Vok-tor has made me think over a lot of things. I cut my hair off because I regret how I treated you mom and dad. You didn't deserve my rejection of you.'

Morgan and Bruce started to cry then.

'Dammit. All of you crying? Ok. Let me get this done. Jyn, I apologize to you because you've made my mom happy, and I hated you for it. I'm still working on that though, so please don't try to hug me. Let's take this one step at a time. Elrek, I apologize to you because there were so many times I wanted to kill you. Just because you were yet another alien that was taking my mom's attention. And she acted positively giddy around you, and well. That just made me sick.'

All of his family started to laugh.

'Great. Now you're laughing. I need to be done with this. Anyway,

'I hated all of you at some point. Even my baby brothers. But mom, my wife is happy. Mandy is happy. You and dad are happy. The only one here that wasn't happy was me. I wanted to shave my head because I wanted to remind myself that things could be so much worse. I have my family, and I have a mission. But before I go back to Earth to fulfill that mission, I had to make amends here. Because when I go, I might not come back.'

Then Morgan couldn't be held back. She went to Alex and hugged him tight. And then he cried into his mom's chest. He finally let go of all the anger that had kept him imprisoned for so long.

When she finally let him go, He said:

'And Elrek, even though you are my Vok-tor master, I need to have a talk with you about knocking my mom up. She can't keep punching out kids for you guys.'

Elrek laughed and said:

'This will be the last one, Alex. Who knows, you may end up training her.' Alex said:

'It's a girl? Crap, Elrek. Don't you have enough of those already?'

Everyone laughed at this. Then Jyn said:

'This is the most precious gift I could have received. Alex, I was so sad to be in your presence because all I could see was disgust in your eyes, and I could feel your hatred of me. Then after a while, it became indifference, which is almost worse than the hate. And now. I feel acceptance. And if that is all I ever get, it will be more than enough. And seeing you like this, with your hair shorn, is honorable amongst my people, and shows more maturity than you know.'

Alex sat quietly for a moment. Then he looked at his mom, caught her hand and said:

'What do you guys have to eat around here? I'm hungry!'

JYN HAD BRUCE MEET him for lunch a few months after they arrived on Prymiah. Morgan was starting to show a baby bump, but still not due for another 6 months. He wanted to speak with Bruce before things got too active with the council and they were already starting to fire up.

'Bruce, I wanted to speak with you alone because of your relationship with Kilra.'

'Yes, she told me she was going on a mission, but didn't tell me where.'

'She also is the only council member opposed to Morgan taking her seat.'

'Well, surely everyone here doesn't agree on everything all of the time.'

'No. But because we are empaths, we try to understand each point of view and usually coalesce for the greater good. Because most of us want to end colonization, we are in favor of Morgan taking her rightful place as the head of the council. But Kilra had another motive.'

'What was it?'

'She became angry because Morgan took me away from her.'

'Were you together before all this?'

'Not in the sense you are thinking. I was the High Admiral of the Colonization Fleet. She was my second and held a great deal of power in that position. And she loved serving as a concubine. I gave her quite a few liberties in that position. Mik is her commanding officer now, and he is a traditionalist like she is, but he keeps a tighter rein on her. She feels constrained. And she feels that I betrayed her because in the beginning, I wanted to capture Morgan so I could possibly become -Shaed.'

'But no one knew she would have twins, right?'

'Varek knew. And Vek had his suspicions. And since Varek is my brother...'

'He made sure you knew too.'

'Yes. I just didn't count on falling in love. So once that happened, Kilra felt lost. She tried to distract herself with you, and it worked for a while, but eventually she became restless.'

'I could tell. She was getting more distant. I did think it felt like she was bored. Not just with me, but with everything.'

'Yes. So I had Mik keep an eye on her. Since he's a traditionalist, she had no reason to think anything of it. But now there's a problem and its growing. And I want to speak with you about what will be happening in the next few months.'

'Go ahead.'

'Mik discovered that Kilra has been communicating with an agent from Jasic Prime.'

'Isn't that the planet where you first...?'

'Yes. That is the planet where I murdered San. Jasic considers Prymiah their blood enemy and have for hundreds of years. They can't match our military, so they have been looking for ways to seek vengeance. Kilra contacted one of their agents to discuss a plan. They want to destroy us from within to weaken us. They have sent their own people to Earth to sow discord, and because there are people who want to take Earth back with violence, they see an opportunity. But there is one more thing.'

'This keeps getting better and better.'

'Unfortunately. Kilra is helping them mount a plan to assassinate Morgan.'

'What! Well that won't happen!'

'No. It won't. But the threat is real. Kilra thinks that by assassinating Morgan, it will appear that the goddess has withdrawn favor from our Revered Mother, and then we will go back to colonizing and I will return as Admiral of the Fleet. In that way, she can have things back to the way they were.'

'Sounds like she's lost her mind.'

'In a sense, she has. Falling in love with you has scared her. Instead of changing her mindset, she is running away from her feelings. But she has committed treason against her people, and because Morgan is the Revered Mother, she has committed heresy as well by planning to have her assassinated.'

'What do we do?'

'Mik is going to keep an eye on her. He is already monitoring her communications. But Alex, Elrek, and I will need to go to Earth soon. We need to formalize a faction of rebels before the discord gets out of hand.'

'Who will protect Morgan?'

'You of course, along with Varek and the Temple Guardians, headed by Vek. She will be quite safe, I assure you.'

'Yes. I have seen them spar. They are lethal. What will happen to Kilra?'

'She will be executed.'

Bruce was immediately saddened by this. His relationship with Kilra was always a bit strange. But he loved her in his own way, and thought she was happy with her circumstances.'

'I know this is difficult, Bruce. I love Kilra, too. She just got lost in all the changes. We may seem like strong people to you, and generally we are. But we are just people with the same flaws as any other residents of the galaxy.'

'When will we speak with Morgan?'

'In a couple of weeks. I will prepare her to address the council. And then we will move forward.'

KILRA WAS GIDDY WITH excitement. She finally got an audience with the Prime Minister of Jasic Prime, although she had to be captured to do so. A few of his men had her while she was held captive. She didn't mind at all. She was getting her fill. And when she got her revenge, it would be even sweeter. Besides. If everything went according to her plan, she would be back to slit each and every throat that touched her. And Jyn would be by her side, where he belonged.

'Kilra-seae of Prymiah Superior! Well, well. I am impressed that you are still standing upright after spending some time with my men. They have enjoyed spending their thirst for vengeance on you. But I know you cunning creatures. You are not captured easily, if at all. What does your filth want with our honorable people?'

'With all due respect, I have something that you desire more than anything this galaxy has to offer, Prime Minister.'

'There is nothing you have that would interest me, Kilra. Other than bending you over and taking what's left of you. Better than what your people did to my ancestor.'

'You may do as you please with me after I make my offer. But I assure you it will be more than what you could ever get from me.'

The Prime Minister was curious as to what this lone Prymiahn could offer him. So he listened.

'Go on.'

'We owe your people a blood debt. We have acknowledged it, and it is common knowledge. And you have sworn to be our enemy until there is nothing left of our alliances. Well. It is also common knowledge that you have no way to exact your revenge without our fleet wiping you out.'

The Prime Minister stood and strode over to Kilra, grasping her by the throat. He let her go when he realized there was no fear in her eyes whatsoever. This made him curious.

'Kilra, you intrigue me, although your people are nothing more than whores. Continue. If what you say pleases me, I may let you go.'

Kilra continued:

'Destroy us from within. There is a movement on Prymiah to end forced colonizations. This cannot be allowed.'

He looked at her curiously.

'What do we care? We want to see that as well. It is the reason for our hatred of your kind.'

'Yes. But listen. We now have a High Priestess on our world that has inspired most of us to stop colonizing. But she has yet to understand her power. It would only take her being removed to cause Prymiahns to question the will of our goddess. It would mean that the doubt created by that removal would create an inner chaos. And while the turmoil is brewing on home world, you can take a part of your revenge on its newest colony-Earth. Only one scout ship protects it. Just think of it. Your fleet could go to Earth and destroy it before Prymiah could save it. It would demoralize Prymiah and have the people believe we should go back to how things were. Not only would you have tasted a portion of your revenge, but you would have more negotiating power with our people.'

'Hmm. Sounds almost *too* reasonable. Why are you doing this?'

'The Revered Mother's -Shaed is my former commanding officer. I had great privilege as his second. It was my hope that I would share in power once he became -Shaed. Now, I must serve another commander, and he is less than liberal with my activities.'

'So this is revenge to you as well?'

'Yes.'

'I see. You are as treacherous as I assumed. But tell me. How do we remove this Revered Mother of yours?'

'I will tell you how to get to her. Then you will send an assassin to kill her.'

'Quite risky. My assassin will need to be compensated. And if he is killed in the process, his family should receive twice his reward.'

'He will get more than he would ever require.'

'I will think this over and let you know in the morning. But I can assure you, this plan has enticed me. Guards, take her back to her cell. Don't touch her. Bring her to me in the morning. Either we'll go with her plan, or I will slit her throat.'

The Prime minister was bent on revenge. His whole planet was. Their ancestors had made a blood oath to avenge San's death by the hand of Jyn hundreds of years ago. Even her death didn't stop the colonization. And the fact that the Prymiahns were not able to completely influence their thoughts to comfort the colonized did not stop them either. Their women were subjected not only to impregnation, but rape. And the remnants of that moment in their history changed them from a relatively peaceful people to one prone to debauchery and lust. He could never change their destiny, but he could avenge it. He decided to go with Kilra's plan. The next morning he summoned her.

'Prime Minister. I see you have your blade drawn. I assume you are going to kill me now and go unavenged.'

'On the contrary, Kilra. I find your plan to be acceptable. But I want to be the one to kill this Revered Mother of yours. It will seal my position as Prime Minister and serve to show my people that I have their best interests at heart.'

'Of course.'

'My blade is drawn to seal our agreement.'

He then made a long cut on his forearm and asked Kilra to stretch out her arm. When she did, he cut hers too, and placed them together. His blood stung her.

'Yes. We have evolved to create venom in our blood. It will leave a scar. You will always be known as a traitor to your people. If we are unsuccessful you will be an outcast.'

'Very well. But I want to be there when you do it. I want to see the shock in her eyes when she draws her last breath.'

'Now. One more thing to seal our agreement.'

'What would that be Prime Minister?'

'Come to my chamber. Some negotiations are best done in private.'

MIK-SEYE, WHO WAS EVEN more treacherous than Kilra, had already infiltrated the Ministry. He told the Prime Minister of what Kilra was planning to do. He knew the Prime Minister lusted for money more than anything else and he offered him a lifetime ransom to go along with Kilra's plan. So the Prime Minister commanded that his men allow Mik to listen and observe Kilra for a share in the king's ransom he would receive. When Mik delivered half of it, the Prime Minister was so excited that he was willing to do anything Mik-seye requested, including listening in on the negotiation. In return, Mik could not interfere with Kilra being assaulted by his men. Mik quickly agreed, knowing that Kilra was looking forward to that almost as much as the assassination of Morgan. He was so angry and disappointed with her. She was going to be destroyed in all of this, but she would not be stopped.

AFTER ANOTHER BORING scouting mission, Kilra had gotten a little too drunk and started speaking to Mik freely.

'Commander, do you ever wish things were like they used to be before the Revered Mother?'

'Kilra, what you are saying is skirting close to treason.'

'Is it? We were fine before Jyn lost his way with her. I enjoyed colonizations. I enjoyed being a concubine. Now look. We are doing nothing but scouting for worlds to negotiate with-not colonize. My skills are going unused.'

'Kilra. You're a seasoned captain. Well respected. You could find a husband easily and settle down. Have some children. You love Bruce, stay with him.'

'I'm bored, Mik! My love for Bruce isn't enough. Every time I'm with him I feel I lose a little more of myself.'

'Maybe you are losing the worst of you and keeping the best.'

'Maybe I want to keep the worst of me, Mik. I miss the way it was before. I intend to get it back.'

'Watch yourself, Kilra. I don't like where this is going.'

'Oh don't worry, Mik. I'm just a little drunk.'

But Mik kept an eye on her after that. And as usual, he was right.

THE PRIVATE NEGOTIATION with the Prime Minister lasted longer than she would have liked. As with the other men on this world, they have developed a way to suppress their release for various reasons. In the case with the Prime Minister, and with his men the previous evenings, it was to make sure she was miserable and in pain before they let her go. Even for Kilra, it was beginning to be too much. But she submitted for the sake of her plan. When he was done, he sat down next to her and gloated at the mess he had made. She was dripping and swollen. Kilra could do nothing but smile as if she enjoyed every minute. It wasn't the sex as much as the smell. She missed her baths. When he left, he told his servants to bring her food and a change of clothes. Then he told her to stay in his chamber while their plans were finalized. When he left, she finally began to cry. Something inside of her told her that this would fail, and that it was useless. She even began to miss how gentle Bruce was with her. But before these thoughts could bear fruit, she thought of Jyn and Morgan, and her anger was kindled again. She would get her revenge. And no matter what, she would have Jyn by her side again.

MORGAN, BRUCE, JYN, Elrek, Vek, and Varek met to discuss the situation with Kilra. It was uncomfortable for all of them. Kilra meant so much to each of them in different ways. And for Morgan, this was especially tender, because she knew how Bruce must feel. Varek started.

'We all know that Kilra has initiated a coup against our Revered Mother, and that therefore extends to the council and to the whole of Prymiah. So we must act quickly but wisely in this. Jyn, have you been in touch with Mik?'

'Yes. He has agreed to pay the Prime Minister handsomely for double-crossing Kilra. But Mik has informed me that the Prime Minister intends to double cross *us* by assassinating Morgan himself. It would seem both the money and his ambition are too tempting. If he succeeds, he will be Prime Minister for life and he would wield enormous power.' Vek continued.

'Yes. So I would like to propose that Morgan, Bruce, Lindsey, Mandy, Johnathan, David, Idra, and Kiisma stay at the residence of the Temple Guardians. There are many secret passageways there that Kilra is unaware of. We can instruct Mik on our plan to lead her and the Prime Minister deep into areas they will be unfamiliar with. I do not wish to disclose much more than that, because Kilra will sense any plan we have to thwart her actions. But Bruce, you play an important role in this, and I must speak with you and Morgan privately.' Then Elrek spoke:

'We sent another smaller scout ship to Earth to begin gathering intelligence and putting our own people in place. Mik was made aware that a very small contingent of Jasic Prime warriors has been sent to sow discord and left last month, but our scouts are faster and will arrive a few months ahead. They will have plans in place for a surprise attack on Jasic Prime's ground troops when their fleet arrives. Morgan, Jyn, Alex, and I will leave after you have our daughter. Idra and Kiisma will take her and the other children for a time to keep them out of danger.' Vek spoke:

'Bruce, beyond what duties I will speak with you and Morgan about, your main concern will be her safety. I want your mind to be focused on that, which I'm sure will be at the forefront of your mind anyway, but Kilra will expect that, and her sensing that in you will not raise any alarms. Morgan, you will be ready. But Varek wants to teach you how to poison a blade. And from what he tells me, you are already quite sufficient with our herbal defenses.' She spoke:

'Yes. I enjoy those lessons especially. But all this is giving me a bit of anxiety.' Vek said:

'Good. That anxiety will shield your deeper thoughts from Kilra. But rest assured, my love. You will not come anywhere near death. You will be in the care of the Temple Guardians, Bruce, and of course, I will not entertain a single hair on your head to be abused. It is my understanding that Bruce is quite proficient with the long blade, so you will sleep soundly. The rest of this business is in the hands of the fleet commanders-and their captains. And Alex is in for a surprise. He must learn to pilot one of our scout ships. He will need to as rebellion leader.'

Bruce and Morgan just shook their heads in unison. Varek asked:

'Something...?'

Bruce said:

'Alex hates to fly, and not only that, he says trying to learn your language is like reading hieroglyphs and he will not respond well to this-*surprise*.' Varek said:

'He'll be fine. He'll adjust to flying. And we are adjusting the translator and controls so he can use Terran words and symbols. We are also fitting it with a cloak and a sleeker design. It does not look like a Prymiahn ship. It looks more like one of the ships of one of our smaller protectorates. If a Jasic Prime ship sees it on their sensors, it will not register as one of ours.' Morgan said:

'Sneaky. Now *that* part he'll love.' Vek said:

'Well, my love, we have been dominant in this sector for millennia. Unfortunately for Jasic Prime, they have overstepped and instead of rightful revenge, they have moved to ambitious arrogance.'

Jyn said;

'But their reason is just, Vek. It is my own arrogance that caused this seed to thrive hundreds of years ago.'

Varek said:

'And you have atoned for that mistake. But we will not leave them in the dust, brother. We will discuss the healing of their wound after this is over. Now let us be done today. We have our plans in place. We must be at peace with the tasks at hand, and we will mourn the dead and soothe our hearts in due time. It is as it should be.'

THE COUNCIL MEETING was outside. It was the most beautiful scene Morgan had encountered. It was under a lovely tree with beautiful pink blossoms. The fragrance delicately covered the whole area. All of the council members were present except for two. Mik and Kilra. The others were couples that attended her wedding. All of the women were pregnant. It was a beautiful gathering.

Jyn and Elrek sat on either side of her, but her Guardian, Vek, stood directly behind her. She found it all to be a bit much, but she also understood this was her duty now. She began as she was instructed.

'It is as it should be. Council of Prymiah. I give you warm greetings.'

'It is as it should be. Revered Mother. We await your words.'

She began. She just wanted to reassure them. So she spoke softly but firmly.

'I thank you for welcoming me home. Your love has blessed me. I humbly acknowledge my need of your help in fulfilling my duty to your world. So this meeting may be different than you are used to. I know each couple serves a different aspect of our culture. Arts, Education, Infrastructure, and so forth. Because I am a newcomer, I feel the need to learn first, and guide later. So as my first duty, I would like to spend time with each couple in their duties, learn what concerns them, what pleases them, and what would make their duties more enjoyable. Then once I have spent time with each couple, we will come together again and discuss. Is that agreeable?'

The assembly was quite excited. Each couple would get to host Morgan and show her the best of themselves. They became quite animated. She continued:

'I see this is agreeable, am I correct?'

Everyone nodded in agreement and smiles.

'Good. Now I also know that there is a disturbance regarding one of our members. I will not speak of it here, as I assume you all know of it. What I will say is that I have deferred the handling of that matter to the Admirals of the Fleet, which is a proper and traditional means of handling such affairs. I am confident that they will resolve this as quickly as possible. It is as it should be.'

'Now let's have lunch and commune together. It's a beautiful day, and I want to start getting to know each of you!'

So the first council meeting went well, even though Morgan was quite glad when it was over. That evening, she and Jyn had an opportunity to speak about it.

'You were wonderful today, Morgan. You seemed so at peace. And the council members have not been this pleased in a while.'

'Why?'

'Our meetings are usually quite stuffy. Empaths already know each other well, so we all know each opinion before we speak it. With you introducing a new method, no one knows what to expect. It's lovely.'

'I'm glad. I hated meetings on Earth. Everyone has their own agenda, and no one is allowed to voice it except those in power. So now that I have a voice, I want everyone to have a chance to speak theirs.'

'I love what you are doing for our world, Morgan. We will never be the same.'

AFTER THE COUNCIL MEETING earlier, Vek was standing some distance away from everyone at the base of a large tree. Morgan excused herself from Jyn and went to join him. He was magnificent in his regalia. And he had loosened his hair so that the golden strands glowed with the reflection from the suns.

'Morgan. You seemed to be comfortable in your position. I am pleased.'

'Well, Vek. I have headed a few committees before. Of course, this was in another life.'

She smiled. Vek said:

'Will you walk with me?'

'Of course.'

'I have a proposal.'

'What is it Vek? You seem uncertain. I'm not used to that coming from you.'

'It is my desire to have you in my bed.'

'Vek. You have established yourself as my mate. Isn't that what that means essentially?'

'You misunderstand. I desire to have you in my bed...as my wife.'

BEFORE RETIRING WITH Jyn, Morgan had a conversation with Bruce.

'Okay. We need to think up a new strategy, Bruce. I think I have gotten myself into this thing too deep, and now I can't control it.'

'What do you mean?'

'Vek wants to be my third -Shaed.'

'I don't see a problem. You seem to have adjusted to our circumstances, what difference does it make now?'

'What are you saying? Have you forgotten the end game?'

'Of course not, but you are also Prymiahn. Doesn't that change how you feel at all?'

'Not in the way you may think. I'm settling into this part of my life. This is true. But Bruce, I just can't forget what was done to Earth. I feel like I'm losing that part of me and if Vek becomes my -Shaed I'll be done for.'

Morgan leaned into Bruce's substantial chest. She seemed supernaturally tired.

'What is it, sweetheart?'

'Vek has a hold on me, and he's powerful. It's as if I can feel him moving around in my spirit, and my body. Since I have a -seae now, its even worse. When we are together, I can't find myself. He says that will go away, but...'

'You don't trust him."

'No. He's possessive. Dominant.'

'I see. You can't control him like you can Jyn and Elrek. *They* love you because you are a gift to *them*. But Vek loves you because he is a gift to *you*. You want the gift. But you think if you accept it, you are his and you don't want to belong to anyone.'

Morgan sat up and looked at Bruce. She had tears in her eyes.

'Lean into me sweetheart. You always have. Now listen. In the beginning of our relationship, before you and I were married, *I* was your Dom. Do you remember?'

'Of course. I needed that in my life. I felt so out of control, but at the same time, I was responsible for so much. I felt tired then. Like I do now. I just wanted someone to take the lead, so I didn't have to.'

'Yes. But after you were healed, that role diminished a bit. We fell in love. But has it occurred to you that you are right back where you started when our relationship began? You are trying to be the puppeteer of a very complex act. You are exhausted. It sounds like Vek desires to take the role *I* did back then.'

'Why can't you do it? Like you did before?'

'Because you are in a different place, sweetheart. You are stronger. More powerful. I can't do what you need me to. Surely you understand this, right?

'Yes. But it's not what I desire.'

'Yes, it is Morgan. You just don't want to admit it to yourself. Remember when we met and had our first experience together? Yes. Your breathing is getting faster, so you remember.'

'Yes, Bruce. I remember.'

'You didn't return my call for a week. But I knew I didn't scare you. You just couldn't believe you enjoyed me dominating you so much. So, I waited.'

'You knew I would call you.'

'Yes.'

'You scoundrel.'

Bruce moved his hand just slightly into Morgan's lap.

'I may have been a bit of a scoundrel. But we enjoyed that aspect of our relationship for quite some time.'

Morgan tried to move.

'Not yet. We're not done. I need to show you something.'

'I'm not in the mood.'

'Don't be stubborn. You know I don't like it when you act out.'

Bruce gathered her dress up to her thighs.

'No Bruce. I mean it.'

She tried to wiggle free. But not too hard.

'Umm hmm. You don't want me to stop. Let me see how close you are.'

He moved his hand between her legs, lightly brushing his fingers against her panties.

'Just what I thought. I feel your wetness through your panties.'

He slipped his hand inside them.

'Bruce...'

'Shh, Be quiet. Open up your legs for me. You know what I want.'

Morgan did what she was told.

'Good. Good girl. You're going to do exactly as I tell you.'

Morgan rose up quickly to her feet.

'I'm not that woman anymore Bruce!'

Bruce stood quickly and grabbed Morgan, she struggled, but he held fast. Then he maneuvered her on face down on his lap.

'Stop being a brat. You always try to fight. It's useless.'

Her dress was already halfway to her waist, so he helped it all the way and slipped her panties down.

'You don't need these.'

He then popped her hard on her bottom, causing her to yell out.

'Fuck you, Bruce!'

Morgan than bit him hard on the thigh which caught him off guard. Then she saw her opening. She caught him by the waist with both arms and threw him to the floor using a Vok-tor move she learned.

Then she straddled his legs and unzipped his pants. Fortunately, he was not wearing underwear. She grasped his dick.

'Look at that! What were you going to do with that? I tell you what *I'm* going to do.'

Morgan, who was truthfully very aroused and very wet, slid herself on his shaft and began to grind oh so slowly on Bruce, causing him to groan.

'There she is. There's my Morgan. Take it sweetheart. It's always been yours. But after you take what's yours, I will have my fill of what's mine.'

But right before she came he flipped her over.

'Now I'm going to finish what you started, since you were so kind as to save me the trouble.'

Afterward, Morgan was shaking, and tears were streaming down the sides of her face.'

'Come here sweetheart. Sit next to me.'

Bruce brushed Morgan's hair off her face and kissed her cheek gently. She rested on his chest again, like she was before. He said:

'Now see? This is who you are now. You remember your power sweetheart. You never lost it. I had to show you years ago, you remember. Now you are more powerful than you ever imagined. And you need someone to show you just how powerful you are.'

'Vek needs to be that to you. You need him to be.'

'But Bruce. What you just did to me...'

'Will not be enough. And besides, our relationship has changed. You know how much I love you. What I would sacrifice for you. We are equals. We always have been. I had to show you that years ago. And when you feel equal to Vek, you will understand the gifts he is trying to give you.'

Morgan finally relaxed.

'Just lay here a moment and sleep, sweetheart. I am always going to be here for you.'

SEEING THE LOOK ON Morgan's face, Vek Continued:

'It's not the title *Shaed*, I am after, my love. It is to be considered by you to be your *shield*. To trust me to protect your heart, mind and body.'

'But, Bruce, Jyn and Elrek serve that purpose, do they not?'

'Not like I can. You know I am not fully Prymiahn. Something else dwells within me. And by transference, to you as well.'

'Yes. I am only beginning to understand.'

'Do you remember when you said to me that you were afraid to meet the goddess because you felt you would be killed if you chose the worship of your god over her?'

'Yes. I remember saying that. But I don't remember my time beneath the Ancestors.'

'But I communed with her while she had you, and in fact, you chose your Terran god- *your* faith-above her, and yet you live.'

'How can that be?'

'For the goddess, it is a matter of faith. She does not require worship or allegiance. But she does require faith. We have many Prymiahns who were children of other worlds. They worship various gods. It is unreasonable for them to worship our goddess, who holds no such requirement of her people. In your commune with her, she found your faith to be profound. As Revered Mother, your faith grounds you to your personal values, and therefore, your integrity. It is a rare thing to maintain faith under the circumstances you have been placed in. Your morals have been tested. You filter all of your actions through the lens of your integrity. Even knowing that we welcome multiple unions as our own sacrament does not free you of questioning the consequences of the heart that come with that.'

'For you to speak that to me, Vek, for you to understand that. It gives me peace to know that you recognize my conflict.'

'Of course, I do. I also know that you are realizing your power. Becoming accustomed to the conflict. Not surrendering to it but understanding your place in it. You understand that you will always have conflict because you are a daughter of two worlds. But your faith, Morgan-your faith is your own. It cannot be taken from you.'

'So if you know this, why must you be my husband? I cannot go through yet another Vrek-mal. And I will not have more children. I cannot, Vek. My soul is tired.'

'Morgan. Remember who I am. You will go through no such trial, as we were bonded long ago. And I need no other child from your being to call my own. Remember, your child will have a part of me within her. She will be quite powerful.'

'A Temple Guardian?'

'Yes. Which is what the goddess requires.'

'What are you saying? Vek, my head hurts. Can we just speak later?'

'Yes. It is difficult. And I am here to soothe all of your hurts. Let me show you.'

Vek began rubbing his thumb firmly at the base of Morgan's neck where there was a tiny node.

'My headache is gone.'

'Yes. There are many things within you that need to be healed. Old wounds, emotional and physical. Even wounds that you received at our own Prymiahn hands that we inflicted on you-not on purpose, but in the ignorance of how precious you truly are.'

'And you believe you can assist with that.'

'Yes.'

'But you don't need to be my husband to do these things. You are already my Guardian.'

'Understand Morgan, I am not asking to be your husband as a gift to you. I am asking you to be my wife as a gift to *me.*'

'And Ysa?'

'Ysa has always loved me, and I will always love her. She has served me beyond what any wife should have to. She has suffered my passions, and they have been abundant. She will remain my wife. But I think she needs some time to remember herself right now, and it pleases me to release her so she may convalesce.'

'Is that usual?'

'No. But I am unique, and in that uniqueness, is a great power. You are the only one equipped to subdue it.'

'Vek. I've only just begun to read the holy script. You have been a Temple Guardian for centuries.'

'Morgan. The script is in the language of the goddess. No one but Varek and I can read those. Did you not notice the difference in the language?'

'No, I didn't, come to think of it. But I did feel like I was in a trance. Like I was drawn to those writings. Its strange. I don't even know how I got to the secret chamber. It was in a deep part of the Temple Library. I wasn't frightened going there. I didn't get anxious until I left and realized what I did. Varek was waiting on me. He had a look of concern on his face, but he was smiling.'

'Yes. We suspected you would be able to read those scripts. But we didn't know for sure. Tell me how you feel right now.'

'I'm fine, Vek. I feel normal.'

'No Morgan. Since you have been speaking with me just now. How do you feel?'

Morgan stayed quiet.

'Morgan. Tell me how you feel. I know already. You must speak it.'

'It seems to me, Vek, that my arousal is increasing the more I'm in your presence.'

'You will be surprised to know that you aren't feeling this way because of the sexual, but what you crave is the exchange of information. Remember? The Ancestors craved knowledge above all else. It just happens that their biology created the conduit for their communication as the sexual act. That is why you are aroused. You have the Ancestors DNA, and now a portion of our goddess. And when we are together, Morgan, you will gain galactic knowledge from me, because the Ancestors and the goddess will use me as *their* conduit. So you see, I need to give myself to you as a gift. I cannot contain it all alone. And your arousal around me is normal for us as mates, but it will consume you if you deny yourself, and I cannot release this knowledge to anyone but you.'

'Vek. I cannot possibly maintain the relationships I have and then add you to the mix.'

'Yes you can. Each of us is unique. And we won't be together constantly. No more than you are with your other husbands. Each feels your need and responds to it in turn, yes?'

'Yes.'

'It would be only slightly different with me. At first our need for each other will be excessive. But soon, Jyn and Elrek will be gone for some time. It will be just Bruce and me to serve you. Bruce is preoccupied with Idra and will be for a while. So you and I have plenty of time to quench each other's thirst.'

'Oh Vek. What do I do? This is too much.'

'You accept my proposal. I will be in the Temple this evening. If you are in my bed when I return in the morning, I will take that as an acceptance. Because I am Temple Guardian, that will be enough to seal our marriage. Only Temple Guardians may share each other's beds. And my invitation to you is sealed if I find you there in the morning. And I hope to find you there.'

BACK IN HER RESIDENCE, Morgan could do nothing but sit and stare at the picture of her and Bruce that she kept inside her journal pages. She felt alone. Bruce was taking care of Idra, and both Jyn and Elrek were planning the long voyage to Earth. She couldn't speak to Alex. He would try to kill Vek. He knew that they had been together of course. But if she told Alex she was going to take on another husband, he would blow a gasket. Lindsey would just be excited and cheer her on. She was sweet like that. And adventurous. But she felt her desire for Vek growing into something otherworldly and strange. And she knew those feelings would not pass. She allowed herself to cry for the first time in a long while. She wanted so much to go back to her old life. But there was no going back. She put on the prayer robe that Varek gave her to study in and walked to Vek's residence.

Prymiahns don't lock their doors. So she walked right in. She had never been in his home. It was breathtaking. It was difficult to tell when the inside turned into the outside and vice versa. There were courtyards and gardens everywhere. It was softly lit, and smelled wonderful, like guests were expected. And when she went into the sitting area, there was a flask of hot tea and a cup sitting on a small table with one cushioned chair beside it. She smiled at this touch. The tea was made of the Guardian fruit. Just what she needed. She sat to take it all in, and slowly sipped the tea. She immediately felt calmer.

After, she finally found what must be the bedroom he shared with Ysa. It was expansive and opened on three sides to a complex garden. A warm breeze was blowing in bringing the scents of the flowering trees in with it. And the large bed. Yes. That was the area that gave her shivers. She decided to take a bath. It would be lovely to bathe alone.

Once she was done, she dried herself but remained nude. She knew there would be no need for clothing. But she still didn't understand why she was so nervous. It was worse than it was with Jyn or Elrek. There was a knot in her stomach. But after she took a few deep breaths, she felt better. It was already getting quite late. So she slipped beneath the covers. She couldn't help but notice the faintest scent of honeysuckle. She fell quickly into a deep sleep.

She woke up on her side with Vek sleeping soundly behind her. His arm was draped across her midsection, and as he breathed, she could feel the swelling of his folds. His breathing was steady and relaxed, so she fell back to sleep.

Sometime, very early in the morning, they both stirred awake and just lay there. Looking at each other.

Morgan whispered sleepily:

'Good morning, my Shaed.'

Vek, upon hearing his new title on her lips, took her hands and kissed them.

'Let me bathe you, Morgan. Then we'll eat and I'll show you your new home. After, I will show you the universe.'

'How will that be possible, Vek? You have shown me so much already.'

Vek paused and smiled at Morgan warmly.

'The golden etchings on my body and yours- are intergalactic maps.'

Don't miss out!

Visit the website below and you can sign up to receive emails whenever Addison Foxx publishes a new book. There's no charge and no obligation.

https://books2read.com/r/B-A-GAOP-TEZUB

BOOKS 2 READ

Connecting independent readers to independent writers.

Also by Addison Foxx

The Revered Mother Of Prymiah
The Savage And The Saint
Serpents in the Temple